A BOND OF BLOOD . . .

The church clock started to toll midnight just as we reached her. Steve leaped out and knocked the pointed piece of wood out of her hands. He pulled her into his arms and let her cry.

He was in love with a vampire, and she'd been enough in love with him to try to kill herself the *only* way a vampire could be killed—by driving a stake through her heart on a crossroads at midnight.

Bad enough to be in love with a vampire, but to be a vampire in love with a normal human being . . .

THE
SQUARE ROOT OF MAN

William Tenn

A Del Rey Book

BALLANTINE BOOKS • NEW YORK

A Del Rey Book
Published by Ballantine Books

To my mother, Millie Klass Levine,
who has always insisted that my lies
be both believable and interesting

CONTENTS

AUTHOR'S NOTE:

Examining this collection, which contains most of my earliest as well as a couple of my latest stories, I was sorely tempted to do complete rewriting jobs. There are stories here written when I was desperately attempting to become a commercial hack, not yet aware that I totally lacked the necessary talent. There are stories here written in the tough, gag-a-minute style then so popular in the magazines and very far indeed from what I have come to realize I do best. ("Your destiny," my friend Rouben Samberg explained to me about this time, "is a very special one. God intended you to starve for art in the pulp magazines.") With what I now know about writing and myself, it seemed to me, I had to make changes.

Then I remembered Aldous Huxley's foreword to the later editions of *Brave New World,* his comments on "the artistic sins committed and bequeathed by that different person who was oneself in youth." This collection is certainly no *Brave New World,* but if I rewrote, as Huxley said of himself, I should probably get rid not only of some of the faults of the story, but also of such merits as it originally possessed." Like Huxley, I decided to resist "the temptation to wallow in artistic remorse." Like Huxley, "I prefer to leave both well and ill alone." I wrote these stories and I was terribly proud of them once: let them be.

My first story, "Alexander the Bait," was written three months after the end of World War II and about eight months before Belmar Labs got the first reflected signal from a radar beam aimed at the moon. I was working as a technical editor for the Army Air Force then, and few reputable scientists I knew envisioned close-up pictures of the moon's surface earlier than a century hence, if ever. I believe this is the only science-fiction story to predict that space travel would be achieved on an institutional basis, rather than by an individual scientist who would build the first star ship in his backyard laboratory. I must admit, however, that my historical parallels were badly chosen, in the event: I went back to economic problems in the age of Columbus; I would have been better advised to have considered matters of gunpowder and cannon.

Like "The Jester," which was written at the dawn of the Television Years, "Alexander the Bait" is today more of a curiosity than a prophecy. Its time will never come to pass. It represents the excitement and imaginings of the science-fiction world a decade and a half before Sputnik and Mariner. Isaac Asimov has described that excitement and that world in his moving essay, "The Lovely Lost Seas of Luna."

For all I know, the worlds of "The Last Bounce" and "Confusion Cargo" may yet come to pass. These two stories are my only ventures ever into classic space opera; both were written in my twenties and are professional versions of stories I first set down at the age of thirteen, the initial impact of *Mutiny on the Bounty* being of course responsible for the earliest draft of "Confusion Cargo."

"My Mother Was a Witch" and the last story in the book are included here only to give the nearer side of the generation gap. One is essentially memoir and the other pure tale; one barely verges on fantasy and the other barely touches science fiction, but these examples of my later work were deemed acceptable to my earlier and much more generous self.

—State College, Pennsylvania
March, 1968

ALEXANDER THE BAIT

YOU AREN'T likely to get a quick punch in the face these days by professing admiration for Alexander Parks. Time has softened even the families of the crews who rode the GA fleet into nowhere; and uncomfortable understanding of the great thing the man did has increased with the years.

Still, he is penalized by a hidebound agency in a manner that, to him at any rate, is especially horrible. I refer to the FLC. I hope they read this.

We wandered into each other a couple of years after the war to end isolationism. I had just landed a Toledo accordion on a freight runway and was now headed for a bar. There are some pilots who know just how much rye they need after towing an accordion; me, I just keep pouring it down until my heart floats back into place.

A cab came up to the flight building and a well-built man with a surprisingly small head got out. As I ran up to hail the cab, the man turned and stared at me. Something familiar about that shoe-button skull made me stop.

"Were you in the Army Air Forces?" he asked.

"Yeah," I answered slowly. "The so-called Swasticker Squadron. Forty—Alex Parks! The voice with a dial!"

He grinned. "That's right, Dave. For a minute I thought you were only talking to ex-flying officers.

Ground control people carry a lot of inferiority complex around with them. You're looking well."

He looked better. The clothes he was wearing had been designed by a tailor with the salary of a movie executive. I remembered something from the newspapers. "Didn't you sell some invention or other to some corporation or other?"

"It was the Radar Corporation of America. Just been capitalized. I sold them my multi-level negative beam radar."

"Get much?"

He pursed his lips and let his eyes twinkle. "Oh, a million five hundred thousand dollars."

I opened my lips and let my eyes bug. "A lot of dough. What're you going to do with it?"

"A couple of unholy scientific projects I've always dreamed about. I might be able to use you." He motioned to the cab. "Can we go somewhere and talk?"

"I'm on my way to a bar," I told him as the cab got under way. "Just came in with an accordion."

"Accordion? Is that what you freight pilots call these glider trains?"

"Yeah. And if you want to know why, just think of what happens when you hit an air pocket. Or a sudden head-wind. Or a motor stall." I grunted. "We make music —heavenly music."

We sat in a back booth of the Matched Penny Café, Alex smiling admiringly as I consumed half the amber output of a good-sized distillery. "You'll have to cut down on that guzzling if you come with me," he said.

I finished the glass, licked my teeth, my lips, and sighed. "Where?"

"A mesa in Nevada I've purchased. Have to have someone I can trust to fly equipment in and help around the place with some moderately heavy construction. Someone I can trust to keep his mouth shut. A heavy drinker keeps his open too much to suit me."

"I'll do that," I assured him. "I'd drink nothing but curded yak milk to get out of this aerial moving van business. Making an occasional trip will be nothing compared to my daily routine with collapsible coffins. It's the combination of monotonous grind with the angel of death that's making me bottle-happy."

He nodded. "And the lack of any long-range useful goal. You flew on almost as rigid a schedule during the war, but—well, that was war. If there were something fine for which you were risking your life, instead of the transportation of electrical harmonicas—"

"Like interplanetary travel? That was one of your bugs. Going to do some experimenting along that line?"

Alex slid his forefinger along the green marble table top. "I'd need much more money than that. It's a nice thought—the human race finds itself at the point today where a little research, a little refinement of existing techniques, would send it to the stars. But the people who could do it, the big manufacturing corporations, can't see enough incentive; the people who would do it, the universities and research foundations, can't see enough money. We sit on this planet like a shipwrecked sailor on a desert island who sees a pair of oars in one spot and a boat in another and can't quite make up his mind to bring the two together.

"No, not interplanetary travel. Not yet. But something along that line. That beam I discovered gave me the reputation of the world's greatest radar expert. I intend to build the largest installation ever on that mesa—and make a long-distance radar survey."

This wasn't the Alexander Parks I'd known. This idea, I decided, showed nothing of what I'd always thought he'd do if he had the money to indulge his sardonically soaring mind, his genius for subtlety. "A radar survey?" I asked weakly.

His little head grew wide with laughter. "A map, my dear Dave—a topographical map of the Moon!"

Nevada was nice. Plenty of landing space. Plenty of working space. Practically no one to ask questions. Sharp, fragrant air on the top of Big Bluff Mesa that affected me almost as strongly as hooch used to. Alex claimed atmospheric conditions here were perfect for maximum equipment efficiency.

The equipment was odd. Of course, I knew radar had developed enormously since the days of primitive gadgetry in the early forties. Parks' own MLN Beam had successfully fused communication and noncommunication radio into a fantastic set-up that required no transmitter and made it possible to tune in on any outdoor event in the world. (It was still in production then.)

Alex and I got the shacks built ourselves, but we ran into trouble with the huge horizontal antenna and the gyroscopically stabilized dipoles. In the end he hired a man named Judson from Las Vegas. Judson did odd jobs around the place and supplied an extra pair of hands in construction jobs. Mrs. Judson cooked our meals. Alex admitted the necessity for Judson, but seemed to regret it nonetheless. I suspected he sent me on sleeveless errands now and then, as if to keep me from having a coherent knowledge of his methods. I shrugged at that thought. If he thought I knew enough about modern radar, I was highly complimented.

When I flew in with a rattling glider train of impossible coils and surrealist tubes, he often insisted I stay put while he made some infinitesimal adjustment in the lab shack. I could climb out of the plane, then, but only if I went directly to the hut which was our living quarters.

Emmanuel Corliss, of the Radar Corporation of America, begged a ride from me once. All the way to Nevada he sang Alex's praises; he told me of the statue of Alex in the foyer of the corporation's skyscraper in Manhattan; he even had a copy of an unauthorized biography titled *Alexander Parks—Father of Global Communication*. He said he wanted Alex to come back as chief research consultant. I thought atomhead would enjoy having his ego caressed.

I was wrong.

Fifty miles from Big Bluff, a deep voice rattled the reception panel. "Who's that you're talking to, Dave?"

Corliss piped up. "Thought I'd look in on you, boy. We might be able to use whatever you're working on now."

"Well, you can't. The moment you land, Dave, unhitch the gliders and fly Mr. Corliss back to the nearest airport. Got enough fuel?"

"Yep." I was embarrassed. Felt like a neighbor overhearing a newlywed couple's first quarrel.

"But, Parks," the executive wailed, "you don't know what an important figure you've become. The world wants to know what you're doing. Radar Corporation of America wants to know what you're doing."

Parks chuckled. "Not just yet. Don't get out of that plane, Corliss, or you'll get a load of buckshot in the most sensitive part of your upholstery. Remember, I can call you a trespasser."

Corliss sputtered angrily. "Now you listen to me—"

"No, you listen to me. *Don't get out of that plane* as you love your swivel chair. Believe it or not, old man, I'm doing you a favor."

That was sort of that. After I'd deposited the red-faced corporation president, I bumped down to the mesa pretty thoughtfully. Alex was waiting for me; he looked thoughtful, too.

"Don't do that again," he told me. "Nobody comes out here until I'm ready for, well, for publication. I don't want strangers, especially scientific strangers, poking around in my layout."

"Afraid they'd copy it?"

My question tickled him. "That's it ... almost too exactly."

"Afraid I'll copy it?"

He threw a quick, shrewd glance at me. "Let's have supper and do some talking, Dave." He put his arm around my shoulders.

While Mrs. Judson dealt out the plain food very plainly prepared, Alex studied me in the hard, unwinking fashion he had. I thought again that he resembled nothing more than a miniature camera set on a massive, unwieldy tripod. Grease-stained blue jeans had long ago replaced the soft sartorial perfections in which I'd first seen him. The father of global communication!

He looked covertly at Judson, saw that the hired man was interested in nothing but his stew, and said in a low voice: "If you feel I distrust you, Dave, I'm sorry. There is a good reason for all this secrecy, believe me."

"That's your business," I told him shortly. "You don't pay me for asking questions. But I honestly wouldn't know an oscillator screen from an indicator rack. And if I did, I wouldn't tell anyone."

He shifted on the hard wooden bench and leaned against the metal wall behind him. "You know what I'm trying to do. I send a high-frequency beam at the Moon. Some of it is absorbed in the ionosphere, most of it gets through and bounces off the Moon's surface. I catch the reflection, amplify it, record the strength and minutest change in direction on a photographic plate, and send another, slightly different beam out immediately. On the basis of multiple beams, I build up a fairly detailed and accurate picture of the Moon from very close range. My multilevel negative radar provides a somewhat stronger beam than science has had at its disposal before, but essentially the principle is basic radar. It could have been done, with a little difficulty, ten years ago. Why wasn't it?"

Stew congealed into an unsavory jelly in my plate. I was interested in spite of myself.

"It wasn't done," he continued, "for the same reason we don't have interplanetary travel, suboceanic mining, grafting of complete limbs from corpses on amputation cases. Nobody can see any profit in it, any *immediate,* certain profit. Therefore, the small amount of research that is necessary to close the gap between the knowledge we already have and the knowledge we almost have goes unfinanced."

"But work goes on in those fields," I pointed out.

"Work goes on, all right. But at what a slow pace, under what heartbreaking conditions! Have you ever heard the legend of how my namesake, Alexander the Great, circled the world astride a giant bird? He hung a piece of meat from a long pole and dangled it in front of the bird's beak. A strong gust of wind blew the meat close enough for the creature to snatch, and the redoubtable Alexander immediately cut a piece of flesh from his side and attached it to the pole. Thus, he was able to complete his trip with the bird futilely trying to reach the meat by increasing its speed.

"The story occurs in several folklores with different heroes, but it shows how fundamental was the ancients' understanding of human motives. Incidentally, it is also a beautiful illustration of the laws of compensation. In every age, a man must offer himself up as bait so that progress will not be limited to the back pages of the dictionary. We can't be said to be moving forward if we touch none of our newer potentialities."

I stirred the stew with a heavy spoon, then pushed it away and reached for the coffee. "I see what you mean. But why tell me all this?"

Alex rose, stretched and moved towards the door. I

smiled apologetically at my coffee and Mrs. Judson and followed him.

The cool Nevada night hung heavily as we walked outside. A myriad stars blazed pinpoint mysteries. Was this black, inviting space man's natural medium, a domain waiting for the flashing tread of a master? Could it be that my puny species was the appointed ruler of these vastnesses? I wondered how it would feel to bank suddenly out there, to level out for a landing. My hands itched for an unmade, still nonexistent throttle.

"These are the maps I've made to date," my employer observed. We were standing in the lab shack with banked transformers, nightmares in spun glass and twisted wire weaving in and out of the huge display tubes around us.

I glanced carelessly at the maps; I was no astronomer. Then I glanced very carefully indeed at the maps.

The point is they weren't maps. They were pictures— over a thousand aerial photographs—taken from a uniform height of about five hundred feet. They had sharper detail than any aerial photographs I've ever seen. You could count the rocks on the surface; you could note pits and the narrowest fissures.

"They are pretty good," Alex said. He stroked one of the glossy sheets lovingly. "A section of the Tycho Brahë Crater."

"Why the Samuel Aloysius Hill don't you publish?"

"Couldn't till now." He seemed to be in the throes of a hard decision. "I had to check something first. And now I've got to trust you with my life's work by asking you to play a particularly dirty trick on yourself. I still can't afford to explain; my conversation tonight was sort of a song and dance to go with the request. But some day it will all fit."

"Go ahead. I'm a loyal employee; I love the firm."

The pinhead seemed to swell. "One week from today I want you to take a trip up to the Canadian North Woods with a couple of packages. You'll have a map with X's scattered over it; the co-ordinates of each X will be marked in the margin. Latitude and longitude in terms of degrees, minutes and seconds. Bury each package about two feet underground at X-designated spots, making certain that it is at the exact intersecting point of the co-ordinates. Then go away."

"Huh?"

"Go away and forget you ever saw those packages. Don't even dream about them. Don't see me except socially for at least three years. Forget you ever worked for me. You can keep the plane and I'll add a sizable check as a parting gift. Will you do it?"

I let my mind chew on it for a while. It didn't make sense, but I knew he'd told me all he intended to. "O.K., Alex, I'll take the high road and I'll take the dough road. I'll make out."

He seemed tremendously relieved. "You will make out— much better than you think. Just wait a few months. When the united savants of the world start flocking in here, there will be lectures and juicy magazine articles thrown at anyone who ever worked for me. Don't touch them with a transmitting antenna."

That made me laugh. "I wouldn't anyway. I don't play those games."

Alex shut off the light and we returned to the Judsons feeling pretty good about each other. That was the way a sweet guy called Alexander Parks climbed up on the altar of history. When I think of the fundamental ambition that drove him to that conversation, the action of the FLC seems cruel and even petty.

A week later I was flitting about the north woods laying little tarp-covered eggs here and there by means of a chart so explicit as to be understandable by grade-school kids.

Newspapers caught my eye when I landed in Seattle. Full frontpage spreads of the pictures Alex had showed me, smaller shots of Alex's small head surrounded by big-browed, white-maned profs from Oxford, Irkutsk and points east.

"Radar Genius Maps Moon," they screamed. "Sage of Nevada reveals work of two years. Scientists flock to mesa, claim telescopes now obsolete except as check. Alexander Parks announces he will make mineralogical survey of lunar surface."

So he had announced it. Good. I spent a portion of my last pay check investigating any new developments in the gentle art of making whiskey. The liquor, I found, hadn't changed; unfortunately, *I* had. Laboring under a diminished capacity, I gamboled from binge to hangover, from bar to hotel room, until I woke up in a hospital surrounded by a straitjacket.

After the doctor had chased the six-headed snakes away, I sat up and chirruped at the nurses. One luscious little redhead took to reading me the newspapers in a pathetic attempt at self-defense. I was getting the news in jerky flashes, what with her dodging around night tables and behind screens, when I heard something that made me reach out and grab the newspaper. The girl, who had been preparing for a last, all-out effort, looked a little dazed.

I still have a hazy memory of that nurse standing in a corner and shaking her head while I got clearance. The doc didn't feel I was cured, but I had important friends.

Bascomb Rockets was the nearest and I was there a half hour after a starchy clerk had given me my clothes, money and a little white certificate, suitable for framing. I'd gone through every newspaper in reach by the time I arrived; so I was prepared for what I saw.

A two-by-three experimental house which had been

operating on a frayed shoestring of a budget was expanding like a galaxy turned supernova. Far off into the distance, I could see shops and hangars going up, stock piles being built, equipment arriving by the cubic ton.

Tim Bascomb was checking blueprints in front of the half-finished Parthenon that was to be the company's main building. I'd met him at an ex-pilot's convention a year after the war, but I thought I might as well reintroduce myself—some insensitive people manage to forget me.

The moment he heard my voice, he dropped the blueprints and grabbed my hand. "Dave! You haven't signed any contracts yet?" he finished anxiously.

"Nary a clause," I told him. "Can you use a former B-29er and accordion player?"

"Can we use you? Mr. Hennessey—Mr. Hennessey, get me contractual form 16, no, better make that 18. You were in on the early jet and rocket jobs," he explained. "That puts you into an advanced category."

"Hiring a lot of the boys?"

"Are we? Every backyard gadgeteer in the country is forming a corporation these days and we're keeping up with the best of them. They say the airlines are using hostesses as co-pilots and candy butchers as radiomen. You'll find Steve Yancy and Lou Brock of the Canada-Mexico Line in that shack, over there; they'd like to see you."

Mr. Hennessey and a stenographer served as witnesses. I started scribbling my name on that contract as soon as I saw the numbers after the dollar sign under "salary." Bascomb laughed.

"I'll back our payroll against any in the world. Not that at least fifty other companies don't do as well. We've got the backing of Radioactive Metals and the Ginnette Mining Corporation as well as a government subsidy of five million."

I wiped some blue-black ink off my fingers. "Since when is the government interested?"

He chuckled. "Since when?" We began walking to a huge structure labeled "Bascomb Rockets Experimental Pilots—No Admittance to Unauthorized Personnel." "Look, Dave boy, when Parks took those radar snapshots of the Moon, the astronomers were interested. When he worked out a spectroscopic table and found there were healthy hunks of gold under the surface, the banks and mines began to sit up. But when that Caltech prof turned Parks' gimmick along eighty miles of the Moon's Alpine Valley and found alternate layers of radium and uranium, the nations of this planet looked up from atom bomb experiments long enough to harness everybody who knows the Moon is a quarter of a million miles from Earth. It's no longer a matter of the first extraterrestrial explorer becoming a trillionaire overnight, but of folks cooking atom bombs in their kitchens."

I looked at the tractors backing and filling around me; at the cement-sloppy wheelbarrows being trundled by an army of construction workers; at the bare scaffolding of shops rising on every bare foot of ground. This scene was being duplicated everywhere in every state, probably in every nation. Slap some sort of a ship together, solve the problems with any kind of jerry-built apparatus—*but get to the Moon first!*

"It isn't only a matter of national defense, either," Tim was explaining. "We almost have atomic power, in fact, we already have it but not in a commercial form. With the uranium that can be dredged out of the Moon, the old *Sunday Supplement* dream of crossing the Atlantic with a teaspoonful of sand for fuel will come true. General Atomics is devoting half their budget to spaceship research. They may not be the first outfit to set a job down on Tycho, but they sure will bust a gut trying."

He led me into the pilots' shack where a lecture on astrogation was in progress. And that day the only rockets on the Bascomb lot were still on drawing boards!

"The Mad Scramble"—isn't that the name of the definitive history of the period? It was mad. People still remember the first casualties to hit the front pages: Gunnar and Thorgersen getting blown to bits a half-mile up; those six Russian scientists flaming into an incandescence that registered on every astronomical camera pointed at the Moon. Then that wave of reaction sweeping the world toward the end of the decade and laws clamping down on irresponsible corporations and wildcat experimenters.

Even then, Steve Yancy and his kid brother got knocked off on a simple experimental flight outside Earth's atmosphere. No fundamental principle overlooked, we were just building carelessly.

When Parks finally dropped in on us on his way from the Leroy Propulsion Project, we seemed to be getting nowhere fast. That was the Black April, the month of the GA Fleet. Bascomb had discovered I knew Parks personally and begged me to bring him into the firm. "He's just hopping about giving advice to anyone who wants it from him. With his reputation, if he ever went to work for one organization he could name his own price. Try to get him to name it for us."

"I'll try," I promised.

"Of course, I know his basic interest is in radar research. If his machine had stopped with mapping the Moon, every hick college would probably have had an appropriation for a radar telescope or whatever they call it. But since he found uranium in them thar craters, kids are being jerked into research projects as fast as they finish elementary physics. That guy from Caltech—what *was* his name?—who first detected radioactive stuff with Parks' equipment, they say he has to go up to the mesa every time he wants to survey some more moon. He can't get the university even vaguely interested in building a toy for him, and Alex P. won't let anyone near the layout unless he's on the scene holding their leash."

"Yeah." I grinned wryly, remembering the way Emmanuel Corliss had been sent back to his dictaphone. Even when some scientific journals had attacked the tight control he maintained over the world's only lunar-surveying radar, he had retorted angrily that the entire apparatus had been developed and built out of his own brain, time and funds and if anyone didn't like it they could build themselves another. Of course, with every research penny eventually finding its way into spaceship design, he had the only game in town.

Parks laughed when I gave him Bascomb's message. He clambered out of the new-smelling black-and-silver job that I was to take on a shakedown in a week and sat on the curving metal runway.

"No, Dave, I like this being advisory expert to big business in rocket research. I get to travel and see all the different things we're trying. Did you know Garfinkel of Illinois is working on a Cosmoplane—sort of a sailboat sensitive to cosmic rays? I'd rather not get stuck in a job in one corner of this business. After all, anyone may hit it."

"But that isn't like you, Alex," I argued. "You were always the kind of guy who wanted to do things himself. This work isn't right up your alley, it *is* your alley. You're the one man Bascomb Rockets needs, not as a part-time unpaid specialist who hits us once a month on his look-see circuit, but as the director, the co-ordinator of our research. I'm just a stumblebum who can make with a joystick, but you are the guy who'll get us there."

"Ever mention our working together?"

"No." I sighed. He evidently didn't want in. I helped him change the subject. "Nasty—this GA business."

He was staring at the ground. He nodded slowly, then looked up. There were ridges of anguish on his face. "That was Corliss," he said in a low, earnest voice. "He became president of General Atomics six months ago. The idea of the Fleet probably seemed like a good publicity trick."

I disagreed with him. "After all," I pointed out, "the logic was good. Ten ships setting off for the Moon together. When one of them hit a snag, the others could come up and help. In case of an impending blowup, the crews of the threatened ship could be transferred to safety. It was just plain unfortunate that Fouquelles didn't discover the deep space Jura rays until a week after they left. From now on everything we build will be insulated against the stuff."

"Five hundred men," Alex brooded. "Five hundred men and women lost without a trace. Nothing in the papers today about a radio signal, about some debris coming down somewhere?"

"No. They probably got out of control and drifted into the sun. Or maybe the ships—those that are left—are scudding aimlessly out of the system."

He was himself again when I left him at the gate. "Maybe I'll have cracked it the next time I see you," I said. "We're moving pretty slowly, though."

"That doesn't mean anything." He shook my hand warmly. "Man has his heart set on getting off this planet. He'll do it—perhaps sooner than he thinks."

Two months later, Captain Ulrich Gall landed the Canadian *Flutterer III* in Plato Crater, using the double-flow drive. It's high-school history now how Gall lined his space-suited crew behind him and prepared to move through the air lock. How he caught his foot on the ramp, and how his Polynesian "boy," Charles Wau-Neil, hurrying to extricate him, tripped on the lock and shot out onto the lunar surface—thus being the first human to touch another world.

I was co-pilot of the fifth ship to reach the Moon—*The Ambassador of Albuquerque*. I was also the first man to set insulated foot on the lunar Apennines. So I'll have a place in some six-volume detailed history of lunar exploration: "An interesting discovery is credited to a minor adventurer named—"

Well, you know what happened. Toehold, the colony Gall left on the Moon, continued the feverish examination of mineralogical samples. No go. In six months Toehold scientists radioed a complete confirmation of Gall's early suspicions.

There was no uranium on the Moon. No radium. And there was just enough gold to be detectable in the most delicate analyses.

Of course they did find some nice beds of iron ore. And someone discovered rocks beneath the surface from which oxygen and the lighter elements could be extracted with ease, making possible Toehold's present indigenousness. But no uranium!

I was on Earth when the storm of public opinion broke. Financed and encouraged by hysterical corporations, it broke first around the head of a certain California professor of astronomy and buried him. He, it was, who had first announced the presence of radioactive minerals on the Moon as a result of experiments with Parks' radar. Then it turned on Parks.

Remember the headlines that day? "Parks Admits Fraud" in letters as big as the end of the world. "Alexander Parks, Nevada charlatan, explained to the FBI today how he planted transmitters near pitchblende and gold deposits in Canada, co-ordinating his infernal machine with them to make it appear that the impulses were arriving from a given portion of the Moon. 'I never allowed anyone to investigate the machine too closely,' Parks leered, 'and this, with my international reputation as a radar expert, prevented discovery.' "

I scooted for his mesa. There were state police coming out of the woodwork, FBI men being trampled underfoot and what looked like a full infantry regiment marching back and forth. After I'd satisfied everybody that I was a reputable citizen, I was allowed to see Alex. He was evidently a *de facto* prisoner.

Alex was sitting at the plain table, his hands clasped easily in front of him. He turned and smiled with pleasure as I walked in. The man walking puffily up and down the small room turned too. With some difficulty I recognized the face above the purple neck as belonging to Emmanuel Corliss. He tore up to me and peering out of red-rimmed eyes began to grunt. After a while, I interpreted the grunts as *"You* ask him why. Ask him why he did it, why he ruined me!"

"I've told you that at least a dozen times," Parks said mildly. "There was nothing against you personally, nothing against anybody. I simply felt it was time we had interplanetary travel and that greed was a good incentive. I was right."

"Right!" Corliss screeched. "Right! Do you call it right to flimflam me out of three million dollars? I personally invested three million dollars to get what? Iron ore? If I want iron ore, isn't what we have on this planet good enough?"

"Your consolation, Mr. Corliss, in your financial bereavement, is that you have helped humanity to take a major historical step. You will recall that I went as far as using a shotgun in an attempt to keep you from getting involved in my . . . my plans. Beyond suggesting that you record it in your income tax under bad investments, I'm afraid I can't help you."

"Well, I can help you!" The president of General Atomics and the Radar Corporation of America shook a pudgy, quivering finger under Parks' nose. "I can help you into jail. I'll spend the rest of my life trying!" He slammed the door behind him so hard that the shack seemed to move three feet.

"Can he do anything, Alex?" I asked.

He shrugged. The pinhead looked tired. I suspected there had been a lot of this lately. "Not so far as I know. All the development on my lunar radar was out of my own funds. While I gave advice freely to those who wanted it, I never accepted a penny from any corporation or individual. I benefited in no material way from the fraud. My lawyers tell me it may be a tight squeeze, but there isn't anything that can be done in the way of punishment. I'm in the clear. Are . . . are you angry at me?"

"No!" I put my hand on his shoulder. "You've made life worth living for hundreds of us. Listen, Alex," I said softly, "I don't know what history will say, but there are a lot of sky-jockeys who will never forget you."

He grinned up. "Thanks pal. I did try to keep you out of the mess. Name a precipice after me."

We can't go any further than the Moon right now, but I have a dandy little two-man ferrying job—secondhand of course—and as soon as I can scrounge up enough cash, I'm going to fit it with that new triple-flow drive. They say Venus should be in an early geological stage, and that means a lot of whole radium and uranium will be lying about. The first man to get there and stake out a claim would be kinda well-to-do the rest of his life. Yeah, that talk may be just some more sucker bait, but, just think, if it *is* so—

Whatever its original impulses, interplanetary transportation is here to stay. But what of the man responsible?

The Federal Lunar Commission (FLC) has issued a

permanent injunction to all its offices against granting Alexander Parks terrestrial clearance. And unless he stows away on some supply ship, or time heals that particular wound, I'm afraid he'll be a wistful Earthlubber to his dying day.

THE LAST BOUNCE

THERE WASN'T much difference between Commissioner Breen's office and the office of any other memorandum baron in Sandstorm, the interstellar headquarters of the Patrol on Mars. If you've seen one, Vic Carlton decided, you'd seen them all; and, in twelve years of standing at attention during the wet-with-tradition ceremony known as the Kiss of Death, he had seen them all—every last uncompromising whitewashed cubicle. Rooms as friendly as a surgical table.

A few star maps speckling the glare from the walls; a bookcase filled with miscellaneous handbooks and manuals of space; one stiff, thin chair behind the stiff, square desk; and, over the desk, the Scout Roll of Honor—names of 563 men who had laid down their lives in the Service: 563 casualties out of a total all-time roster of 1,420.

Yet the Scouts were a volunteer service, and every year, all over the galaxy, young men broke their backs and overloaded their brains to get into it.

The speech was pretty much the same as usual. Perhaps even better in one way: Breen was new to the job and slightly—well, *embarrassed* by this aspect of it. He kept his talk short; made the Kiss of Death almost a peck.

He was tall and straight as they: he had no more than three years on Vic Carlton, the oldest of the three; and his blue uniform differed from theirs only in the badge of office, a gold star instead of a silver rocket, on his chest.

"Lutz and O'Leary, you are under the command of Victor Carlton—one of the very few men on active duty with over ten years' experience. Carlton, your two juniors have been certified as psychologically, physically, and educationally fit for this mission: no more can be said of any man. I must remind you that the Patrol has been called the glory of space and the Scouts the glory of the Patrol; but I need not remind you how jealously that glory should be guarded. Good scouting, good luck. That is all."

He exhaled a tiny gust of relief before shutting his mouth.

All? Vic Carlton thought, as they saluted and about-faced to the door. *This is only the beginning. You know that, Breen. The danger and the horror—death perhaps, agony without death perhaps—start officially when the commissioner's talk is finished. You should know: you decided you had a bellyfull six months ago and resigned from active duty for this sleek office job. When we walk out of your office, it's only the beginning.*

Then he thought: *Hey, those are dangerous ideas for a commander. Maybe Kay's right; maybe I'm getting old.*

And *then* he thought: *Breen's only thirty-five; I'm thirty-two. I remember when I thought all commissioners were shambling wrecks held together by will-power and a handful of regulations. Why, Breen's only thirty-five! I am getting old!*

They were out in the corridor, and a group of scouts being briefed for another set of missions swung down to the elevator with them. They clapped their helmets on, leaving the broad, flaring visors open.

"Attaboy, O'Leary, take it on the bounce!"

"You don't know how lucky you are, Lutz. Unkillable Carlton is my idea of a commander for a rookie's first mission."

"Look at Carlton, fellows. He's *bored!* What a man!"

"The first bounce is the hardest, O'Leary. Gee, I remember mine!"

"Hey, Lutz, what're you looking so green about? According to statistics, you have an even chance of coming back in one hunk!"

"On the bounce, O'Leary. On the bounce."

Carlton watched his men. O'Leary was the one to look out for at this point. Lutz was still riding the enthusiasm of graduation from the academy; he might be frightened at his baptismal mission, but he was even more exhilarated. He wouldn't be important until action started; and, even then, he'd probably have to be checked from daredevil stunts more than he would have to be encouraged to take a chance. But O'Leary was the one to watch.

It was tough making your first bounce. Vic remembered his—was it nine? No, eleven years ago. A commander who'd been so badly off that he'd requested disenrollment in preference to making a bounce, the other junior so psychologically smashed that he'd become a permanent resident of the tiny Patrol Mental Hospital on Ganymede. A kind of carnivorous moss had almost got them: pretty screaming awful. But Vic had been patched up and made his bounce on the very next mission out of Sandstorm. You had to bounce right back or your nerve would go.

Sure enough, O'Leary sounded off.

"We drew a creampuff. The planet's only three-tenths of a point off Earth-type."

The others hooted at that. "And it's out around the Hole in Cygnus! Where they found a nova acting like a third-magnitude star and a meteor stream traveling at the speed of light! The part of the galaxy that never heard of Newton! You can have it!"

"That region hasn't even been adequately mapped, O'Leary. It may be the place where time warped in on itself and exploded, where the universe got started. A

creampuff, he calls it! You can have it: I'll be happy with a
planet six full points off Earth-type, in a sane area like
Virgo or Taurus or something."

"Sure, don't kid yourself, O'Leary. But on the bounce,
boy, take it on the bounce!"

"Hey, Lutz, what're you looking so green about?"

Harry Lutz giggled weakly and wiped palm sweat off
on his blue jumper. Carlton slapped him on the back,
kneaded his shoulder blades. "Don't worry, you have two
experienced men behind you. We'll take care of you,
won't we, O'Leary?"

O'Leary looked up startled, then nodded seriously.
"Sure; we'll show you the ropes, kid."

Good. Get O'Leary's mind off himself, get him to worrying about the rookie instead, and he'd have no time for
a funk.

The elevator stopped on the main floor of the Scout
Operations Building unimaginatively decorated in azure
plastic. Through the open double doors, Vic Carlton could
see the mob of civilian personnel who always left their
jobs when a mission took off. Death-watch in Sandstorm,
the Scouts called it. Oh, well, he shrugged, it must be
exciting for civilians. Man's empire extends another couple of light-years into space—that was probably exciting
to some people.

Someone started the song—

> Bell-bottomed helmet, suit of SP blue,
> He'll shoot the ether like his daddy used to do. . . .

The three had linked arms when they began singing.
Their feet beating the rhythm, they marched down to the
slender little ship with the long blue stripe that lay waiting
for them at the end of Sagittarius Runway. Behind them,
their honor guard of Scouts bawled the chorus at the pink

Martian sky. On either side, people cheered. Evidently, Vic reflected, this was something to cheer about.

"What about you," Kay had asked last night, after he had hummed the song, lying with his head on her lap and watching the two moons of Mars coruscating overhead. They'd walked in the Rosenbloom Desert for two hours, and when she'd sat down in the coarse red sand, he'd put his head on her lap and hummed the song because he felt so strangely tranquil. "What about you—don't you want a son? Don't you want him to—to shoot the ether like his daddy used to do?"

"Kay, please. Of course I want a son. As soon as we can get married—"

"But you can't. Not while you're on active duty with the Scouts. You can't have a son. The only children that active Scouts have are orphans. That's different, Vic. Orphans who never have seen their daddies."

He grimaced at her brown eyes, certain and serene under the perfect piles of blonde coiffure. "Look, I want to marry you, girl. I'm going to marry you. And I agree with you that we can't build a home life around Scout missions."

"Yes, Vic."

"You're right about my being no good to you—or any woman—until I decide on my own that one planet is good enough for me. You don't want me counting jet-trails wistfully; and you don't want me with all the fire gone out—you said so yourself. I've got to want to build a family as much as I want to scout."

"Yes, Vic."

He made an impatient gesture and cut it short as he watched her draw five parallel trails in the sand with her fingers. "So? So it's just a matter of patience on your part, just a matter of waiting until I'm ready to chuck the whole thing. After all, I've been a Scout for twelve years; the odds against that length of service are pretty high—most men who survive five years of it are ready to quit. You'll have me soon, Kay—and not as a shoulder-shrugging has-been, but a guy who's adventured enough in space and is ready to roost. I'm still young by ordinary standards—only thirty-two. Trip after next, three or four missions from now maybe, I'll be ready. Soon."

A pause. Then— "Yes, Vic." Her voice was low, agreeable.

Somehow, in retrospect, it seemed like the most final of quarrels.

Vic found himself looking for Kay past O'Leary's huge head. She worked in Administration; she'd be in the bunch near the great white dome. He wished he could kiss her before they took off; but tradition demanded that farewells be said the night before and nothing interrupt the march to the ship.

He caught sight of her just as they reached the part of the song that always made her wince. Vic grinned in anticipation.

> If it's a girl, dress her up in lace;
> If it's a boy send the bastard off to space!

She winced so hard, screwing her eyes down and pulling her shoulders up, that they had marched past her and into the ship before she looked around again.

The two regular Patrolmen who were on duty saluted and said, "Ship in good order, Commander. Luck." They left.

The other Scouts gave them one more round of handshakes before climbing silently through the open locks.

Vic pressed the green hexagonal button that shut the air-locks, and, leaping to the portholes, they all took a last quick glimpse of Sandstorm's concrete buildings rising like so many bandaged thumbs out of the rosy Martian plain.

"Jets in good order, Commander," the voice of the ground-crew chief announced. "Awaiting take-off."

"Mission crew ready," Vic told him in the communaphone, as Lutz and O'Leary went to their stations. "Taking off."

His eyes swept around the pilot-room, focused on his juniors for a double-check, came to rest on the clicking gauges.

"Jets away," he said and cut the communaphone connection.

He counted to fifteen slowly, thinking of the immemorial cry of "Jets away! Jets away away, jets away!" that was being sung out on the ground below as the crowd scattered.

"Fifteen," he said, and O'Leary pulled the red switch the requisite two notches, while Lutz swung the tiny wheels of the balance-control. They jerked slightly in the seats, then, as Vic adjusted acceleration helix, they relaxed comfortably. Mission begun.

Mission 1572 on the schedule of the Scouting Patrol; Number 29 in Vic's personal Service Record back in Sandstorm, the last page of which was headed "Circumstances of Death—Posthumous Citations—Provision for Dependents." Not many Service Records could count that high. When a man passed his twentieth mission, they began calling him "Lightning" Ching Lung or "Safety-First" Feuerbach or "Two-Blast" Bonislavski. You had to hang some such nickname on a man who, mission in, mission out, came back with three-fourths of his skin missing or some weird virus that made the medics dither and dream up whole new pathologies—but a man who *always* came back. Until, of course, there was that one time—

They called Vic "Unkillable" Carlton, and there were only two Scouts now shooting the ether who had longer active service. One of his very few ambitions was to be the

Senior Scout of Space and wear the gold uniform that went with the rating. It meant that you never paid for anything anywhere, that you walked through Patrol cordons, that you were practically a one-man parade wherever you went. That would be nice, Vic thought; it was childish and garish, but it gave a man some sort of goal at this stage of his life. It meant that even in the Scouts who were the chosen of the Patrol, in turn the chosen of the galaxy's male population, you were still unique. It also meant that one day you might cut your throat while shaving with a safety razor.

Cute idea, the Scouts. Economical. Instead of losing thirty or a hundred highly-trained scientists at a clip, civilization, at most, would lose three men. True, the three would be rather unusual men with remarkable qualifications; but in a galaxy swarming with youths thirsty for a nice suicidal-type job in adventurous surroundings with a little glory, fair pay and *plenty* of room for advancement, the three would be replaced. And Honor-Rolled.

A Patrol cruiser happens to run across a previously uncharted star which is the one-in-a-thousand with a family of planets. Spectroscopic observations are made; and, if the cruiser has the time, robotjets are sent out to circle one or two of the more likely-looking worlds and make automatic observations on their atmospheres, ground conditions, evidences of intelligent life and the like. If there are no signs of an indigenous civilization anywhere, the cruiser goes on about its business and reports its findings to Sandstorm HQ at the earliest opportunity.

Sandstorm files the information along with a mass of deductions by physicists, chemists and biologists. Five years later, say, it becomes necessary to make a more detailed examination of one of the planets. Maybe the surface promises interesting mineral deposits; maybe it's a good spot for a fueling station or Patrol outpost or a colony; maybe it's just that someone important is curious.

Three available Scouts—one A, one B and one C Scout—are alerted. They are briefed for a month on all data handy, given the best ship and equipment that can be built, wished lots and lots of luck and sent off. If they aren't back in ninety days, Terran time, a heavy cruiser crowded to the stern jets with fancy weapons and brilliant minds goes after them to find out how they were knocked off. If any or all of them return in the prescribed time, their reports are examined and, on the basis of their experiences, an expedition is organized to do whatever job is necessary, from mapping the site of a colony to laying the foundations of an astronomical observatory.

The Scouts are sitting ducks. Oh, sure, their motto is "Take No Chances" and Scout Regulations 47 to 106 deal with safety measures to be observed. They are supposed to wander about the new planet with recording instruments, getting first-hand, on-the-spot data. That's all the books say they're supposed to do. And back in the academy—

"Back in the academy," Lutz confided to O'Leary as, outside the orbit of Pluto, they prepared to switch to the interstellar jets that would sweep them to their destination at several times the speed of light, "back in the academy, they told us three-fourths of all Scout casualties are caused by carelessness or disregard of the safety regulations. The commissioners said that as discipline improves and more men adhere closely to regulations, casualties will inevitably go down."

"They will, huh?" O'Leary glanced round at Carlton and sucked in his lower lip. "I'm right glad to hear that. It's nice to know that casualties are going down. I'll take a commissioner's word against nasty statistics any old time. *Down*, huh?"

Harry Lutz completed his sight and handed the instrument to O'Leary for checking. "Sure. We function simply as an advance-information crew. At the first hint of danger we're supposed to clear out. 'Better lose your bonus than lose your life.' "

"And outside that fat bonus for a full scouting period on a planet, what other compensations are there to this wacky job?" O'Leary nodded at Carlton. "Objective lined up, Vic. We can shoot. You try coming back from a mission with a scarey story, boy; you'll find yourself demoted to watch-dog duty in the Patrol before you can say Aldebaran Betelgeuse Capricorn. Or take that last mission I was on. Nothing dangerous on the planet— nothing, that is, that *wanted* to do us harm. But there was a bird thing with funny wings which generated a high-frequency sound wave as it flew. Pure biological accident, but it happened to be on exactly the same frequency as our supersonic pistols. Yeah."

He breathed heavily and stared through the control levers. The other two men watched him closely. "First time we saw it was the day Jake Bertrand was making a geological survey outside the ship. It flew down and lit on a rock—it was curious, I guess—and Jake dropped dead. Hap MacPherson, the commander, ambled out to see why Jake had fainted. The bird thing got scared and flew away, so Hap dropped dead, too. I was inside the ship and noticed where the sound meters were pointing; I figured it out. After I had me a good round look at the horizon and made sure there was nothing flying anywhere, I dragged the two brain-curdled corpses in and went back to Base. I don't know whether they decided to wipe out the bird things, send a colony down with a new kind of head-shield or what. But they gave me my bonus."

Silence. Harry Lutz started to speak, looked at his companions and stopped. He wet his lips and leaned back in his seat. *"Gee,"* he said at last in a small, wondering voice.

"All right, O'Leary," Vic rapped out. "If you're

through with your Horror Stories for Young Recruits we can move. Stations for interstellar shoot!"

"Station B manned," O'Leary said, grinning so that his teeth showed and the corners of his mouth didn't turn up.

Harry Lutz gulped and straightened his shoulders inside the blue jumper. "Sta-" he started and had to begin again. "Station A manned. Interstellar j-jets away."

Nope, you can't fool the Scouts. They know they're sitting ducks. All the same, Vic decided, Lutz and O'Leary were good for each other. When you made a bounce after a trip where Death had dug a humorous forefinger in your ribs and slapped your shivering back— about the best thing you could find on such a bounce was a younger man who knew less than you did, who needed guiding, whose fear was actually greater than yours because it was latent and had, as yet, hit nothing tangible to set it off.

O'Leary was coming out of himself, thinking less of his own problems and more of the younger man's. And Lutz wasn't being harmed either: if some stories could frighten him enough to make him an unreliable companion, the real thing was no place to discover it. Better find it out now, here, where steps could be taken to protect the other two. In twelve years of Scouting, Vic Carlton had concluded that the only man who didn't scare at what the missions encountered was either too phlegmatic to be useful or else a true lunatic: the normal man was afraid, but tried to handle the source of his fear. Let Lutz find out what they were likely to be up against: his survival chances would be the better for it.

"Oh, it's not such a bad life at that," Steve O'Leary admitted as, the interstellar shoot under way, they were relaxing in the spherical space which served as combination pilot house, living quarters and recreation room. "A month for briefing, two months—at maximum—for the round trip, a month on the planet of mission. If you're lucky, the whole duty period takes no more than four months, after which you get a full thirty days' leave—over and above any hospital time. Pay's good and the glamor-struck women are plentiful: what more can a man ask?"

"Besides," Lutz hunched forward eagerly, transparently glad of his colleague's change of mood. "Besides, there's the *real* glory—being the first humans to set foot on the soil of the planet, the first men to find out what each world is like, the first—"

"That part they can have," O'Leary told him curtly. "The first humans on each world—*hah!* The first *funerals!*"

Vic Carlton leaned back in his plastic chair and chuckled. "What's the matter, Steve—did the commissioner flog you into the ship? You didn't have to make the bounce; you could have disenrolled."

"When I'm only five months away from A Scout rating, double pay and retirement privileges? Not that I'll ever have sense enough to retire: the first O'Leary was a romantic bonehead and the male line has bred true. There was an O'Leary who got himself blown apart in the strato-sphere back in the days when they were trying to ride to the moon on liquid oxygen; an O'Leary was navigation officer on the Second Venusian Expedition one hundred and fifty years ago—the expedition that fell into the sun. Science may come and Invention may go, but the O'Leary's will go on sticking their heads into nooses for-ever. Amen."

They all laughed at his lugubrious nods, and Lutz said: "I only hope all my missions will be as dangerous as this one! The star is a yellow type G, just like our sun, and the planet—"

"The planet's only three-tenths of a point off Earth-type!" the B Scout broke in, his mood shifting again. "I know. That's what I told those jokers back in Sandstorm. But listen, boy, that planet and that star are around the

Hole in Cygnus—do you know what that means? There hasn't been a single planet scouted in that area, let alone colonized. All anybody knows about the Hole in Cygnus are somebody else's theories. Ask any scientist why there are so few suns in the area, why matter behaves the way it does out there, what might have happened to that carto-graphic unit that got itself lost five or six years ago, and he'll tell you to please not bother him. One consolation, though; if we don't come back, there'll doubtless be a full-dress investigating expedition. Makes you feel good, doesn't it, Vic?"

Carlton shrugged, turned back to his book. He couldn't decide which was worse—Lutz with his callowness, his fumbling inexperience, or the older man whose wry humor flowered so easily into bitterness stemming from obvious fear. For such a mission, he thought, the Scouts might have reversed an ancient rule and allowed him, as com-mander, to choose his own men.

Although, on his own initiative, whom would he have chosen? A nice dependable B Scout like Barney Liver-wright who had been knocked off around Virgo six months ago? An up-and-coming C Scout, full of blood and guts, like Hoagy Stanton who was even now dying on Ganymede in a room which the pathologist dared not enter for fear of a virus which might seep through any immunization procedure, any protective clothing?

No, you took what you got, what there was available— what there was still alive. Even on the mission to the Hole in Cygnus, the commander took the men assigned to him, and, Vic thought, watching them as the ship's chronome-ter told the passage of the weeks which only it could record out here in black space, he didn't have such a bad crew at that.

A tight comradeship developed that he had known before. The three men came closer and, despite their cramped quarters and the natural irritations arising from their log-book routine, felt the warmth of friendship.

Lutz in particular became more sure of himself as he was openly accepted by the other two. Vic watched him, his small dark head like a planet beside O'Leary's huge red sunburst as the two men beat out the measures of a sloppily sentimental ballad currently popular among the Scouts. He grinned at Harry Lutz's tearful tenor winding its melancholy around Steve O'Leary's stanchion-shaking bass.

> No more to the stars will I go,
> No more a smooth jet will I know;
> Through spendthrift days, a maiden's praise
> Will hold me in thrall.

> I'll go my ways, and end my days
> On some mould'ring ball.
> No more to the stars will I go—O lads!
> No more to the stars will I go.

It hardly applied to Kay, Vic decided. "A maiden's praise—" That was hardly what he got from her.

Kay was critical: Kay was strength seeking strength, not a limp flag of a female searching for a strong male staff. With her, for the first time, he had begun to examine the internal forces which had driven him into one of the most dangerous and least rewarding services ever organized by humanity.

That night when he'd come tardily to their date outside Sandstorm's swankiest restaurant and said casually, belligerently, "Just signed papers for Mission 1572. Adventure done got between us again, girl."

"There's nothing wrong with adventure," Kay had commented slowly, after turning aside. "Every young man must measure himself against obstacles too big for his fellows. That's how the race advances, that's how new governments are created. It gets to be a perpetuated adolescence when it leads to nothing fundamentally constructive; when it's pursued for its own sake."

"The Scouts don't pursue adventure for adventure's own sweet sake," Vic had growled. "The Scouts have initiated every colony in the galaxy—they've been responsible for every outpost in the stars."

She laughed. "The Scouts! Vic, you're talking of a service; I'm discussing the individuals in it. When a man of your age has nothing more to show for his life but a few scars and a dozen tarnished medals— I only know that as a woman, I want a strong, steady and reliable man. I don't want to marry a boy of thirty-two."

"You're saying," Vic went on doggedly, "that pioneers, revolutionaries and adventurers are not mature men. In essence, you feel that the race advances because of its cases of arrested development. Right, Kay? Isn't that what you really think, that adolescence is the period of experiment and excitement—and maturity, the period of settled stodgy dullness where you cultivate your ulcers instead of your mind?"

He remembered the way she had stared at him, then dropped her eyes as if caught in a fib. "I—I don't know how to answer *that*, Vic. It seems to me that you're talking like a little boy who wants to be a fireman and is secretly very much ashamed of his Dad who works for a fire insurance company, but I could be wrong. I know that with your ten years plus in the Scouts, you could get a commissioner's appointment by asking for it, and that it would be just as exciting to plan missions and prepare younger men for their dangers as rocketing out on them yourself. But I don't want you to give up active duty for me, or even for our possible family, if you haven't grown up enough to want it yourself."

"You mean grown *old* enough, Kay."

She gestured impatiently and turned to examine her hair in the mirror. "Let it go," she said, winding an intricate curl with complete concentration. "I never can see what there is about this discussion that upsets you so. Either you want to settle down and have a family—or you don't. When you decide, I'll be very much interested in hearing from you. Now let's see if Emile's Oasis has that band in from Earth yet."

He held the door open for her, irritably trying to decide why these conversations always left him with the feeling that he had committed some unpardonable social blunder which she had been gracious enough not to comment upon.

Looking back now, he found he still could not be critical. He found himself wondering what he was doing out here, sharing living space with two strangers named Harry Lutz and Steve O'Leary.

What was mission 1572, what was the first scouting expedition to the Hole, as compared to Kay's soft presence and a youngster in whom they would both appear again? The urge that filled him—the hunger to found a family— was incredibly ancient, and every cell in his body had evolved to respond to it. Sitting watchful in the deep control chair, he plucked moodily at his stiff blue uniform.

And then a light in front of him flashed redly.

"Scouts to stations," Vic bawled. "On the double, there —on the double! Star of mission on the point! Stations for switch to planetary jets." He was calm again, and sure of himself: a mission chief.

"Station B manned," O'Leary rapped out, jolting into his seat and pulling a long bank of switches open.

"Station C manned," Lutz's voice was indistinct through the remains of a quiet supper he'd been enjoying in the galley. "Planetary jets away!"

Vic's eyes raked across them, considered the stellar map

spread in front of him, noted the gauge needle palpitating in its circular prison, and checked the relay near his right hand for maximum gap.

And double check.

"Planetary jets away," he called. "Planetary jets away, away. Jets away!"

They came into a system of eleven planets whose sun's spectroscopic reading was remarkably similar to that of Sol. Between the second and third planets there was one asteroid belt; between the eighth and ninth, there was another. Three of the planets were ringed—one both horizontally and vertically like a gyroscope—and only one world, the fifth from the sun, supported life.

"Could swear it was Earth if I didn't know better," Harry Lutz marveled as he looked up from an examination of the mission-planet.

O'Leary nodded. "Three-tenths of a point off Earth-type is pretty close. Slightly small diameter, oxygen and nitrogen balanced almost on the dot, only two degrees difference in the average equatorial temperatures. And *still* the exploring ship couldn't find any evidences of intelligent life. Hey Vic—according to Cockburn's Theory of Corresponding Environmental Evolution, shouldn't there be a creature down there who, at the least, approximates paleolithic man?"

The A Scout, wearily watching the transvisor click off the remaining million miles, moved his shoulders up expressively.

"I could give you a guess anywhere but in this gap in the wide open spaces. Sure, the biology of a planet that close to Earth physically should have produced an intelligent biped with the beginnings of a machine civilization—but who knows about the Hole in Cygnus? Take those white horrors out there."

They followed the direction of his arm pointing up at the planet-studded telescanner. Here and there in this system, between planets and upon them, floating free in empty space and clustered about the yellow primary, were seemingly tiny networks of white, dead-pale filaments extending for what were actually hundreds and thousands of miles. Like the broken webs of immense and ugly spiders they looked, uninterested in gravitation and resembling nothing in a logical cosmos.

"Don't try, Harry," Vic warned Lutz, who was feverishly leafing through an immense volume on the control desk. "You won't find them listed in Rosmarin's *Types of Celestial Bodies*. All that we know about those things is that they are there—everywhere in the Hole—and they're too dangerous for the best stuff we've been able to make up to now. Any ship that gets too snoopily close to them, goes out—pouf! It just isn't around any more. Our orders are: MAKE NO ATTEMPT REPEAT IN CAPITALS UNDERLINED MAKE NO ATTEMPT TO EXPLORE WHITE CLUSTERS AND ANY OTHER PHYSICAL MANIFESTATIONS PECULIAR TO HOLE IN CYGNUS."

O'Leary snorted. "That's just this trip. After we get back (*if* we do) someone at Base will scratch his head and wonder what those white clusters can possibly be made of. So they'll shake our hands, give us a couple of box lunches and a new ship, and say 'Would you mind looking into this matter and seeing if it is really as dangerous as rumored—taking no unnecessary chances of course? And it would be sort of nice if one of you could make it back in time for the Solarian Convention of Astro-Physicists in January!'"

They guffawed, Lutz on a slightly higher note than the other two.

The planet was enough like Earth to bring on a severe case of homesickness. True, there were only four continents, and true, there was no dainty moon reigning over the warm nights; but the seas were sapphire enough for a man to lie on their white beaches with a bottle of whiskey and get drunk without opening the bottle, and the clouds pushed their curling bellies across a subtly tinted sky unaware of the glorious things poets could do with them. Here and there, a perfect island poised above the noiseless indigo waters, waiting for a painter to whom to give itself.

Tall trees boiled up the sides of mountains, lush grass waved on the uncombed prairies. Deserts sweltered their immense length of golden moistureless sand; and, in the north, a huge ice floe precipitated spring by plunging into the polar sea with a wild shriek of freedom.

But on all the land, and in all the seas, they saw no living thing move.

"Like the Garden of Eden," Harry Lutz breathed, "after the Fall."

O'Leary looked at him, bit his lip. "Or Hell, before it."

After they landed, Vic assigned investigative watches. Much easier than the nerve-wracking space watch, the investigative watch was, at this stage of their mission, much more crucial. Both Scout Regulations and their own appreciation of safety-first methods demanded that the most painstaking examination possible be made of the planet while they were still inside the ship. Not only did the ground have to be checked for such topographic capers as earthquakes, floods and volcanoes, not only did the possibility of dangerous sub-microscopic life require careful consideration on so Earth-like a planet; but also— especially here in the Hole—they must be on the lookout for the completely alien, the peculiar deadliness without precedent—up to now.

Not until all these precautions had been taken and the log-book carried to the moment of landing did Vic realize he hadn't thought of Kay for ten—or was it fifteen?— hours. Kay Summersby was just one more blonde adventure that hadn't quite worked out, another backdrop in his memory—a little more important, a little more protracted than the rest. His only responsibility was the mission.

"Hey, Vic," Steve O'Leary frowned up from the tele-scanner. "Do you know there's a white tentacle thing on the other side of the planet?"

The mission commander grunted, moved to the side of the B Scout and scratched his chin at the instrument.

"Black Space!" he growled. "What would you call it? Doesn't seem to be alive, doesn't move, doesn't have any visible connection with the ground; just hangs there, hurt-ing the eyes. Makes me think of an unhappy hour some-one ripped up and threw away."

O'Leary pulled at his fingers. "Yeah. I don't like it, and I don't want to see it. According to regulations, we're supposed to stay at least a full jet-trail length from these babies—and here this thing is a stinking 7500 miles off in a straight line through the planet."

"That's just our own bad luck," Carlton told him. "It's on the planet of mission, and our mission orders always move ahead of Scout Regulations. Just remember to keep your distance on exploratory trips. Hear that, Lutz?"

The C Scout nodded. "When do we start the trips, Vic? If there's anything dangerous on this unearthly paradise, I'll eat my helmet from the antenna down. I'd like to feel some ground slapping at the soles of my feet."

His superior shook his head.

"Take it easy, boy, take it slow and easy. On a strange planet, all you get for hurrying is a sooner grave than your neighbor. And if there's anything dangerous on this world that you don't know about when you step out of the lock, why, you won't have to eat your helmet. Because it will eat you, helmet, radio phones and all. Now relax and get back to that telescanner. There must be *something* alive here besides trees, grass and potatoes."

But there wasn't. At least they couldn't find anything though they spelled each other at the telescanners, nudged the beam back and forth over the four continents and peered at the screens until their eyes writhed with fatigue. They found minute one-celled forms in the specimens of air, soil and water the ship's automatic dredges picked up; O'Leary's shout brought the other two tumbling out of their bunks the day he thought he saw a bird (it turned out to be only a leaf tortured by the wind); and a few large green balls they noticed scudding about excited their interest until the scouts decided from their aimlessness and lack of sensory apparatus that they were over-large spores of some plant.

They saw no herbivores cropping the rich vegetation, no carnivores slinking behind them for a spring. The seas held no fish, the woods no termites, the very earth itself no earthworms.

"I don't get it," Vic growled. "The botany of this planet is sufficiently close to Earth's to indicate a terrestrial zoology. Where is it? There's no creature out there large enough to have eaten all the others. So-o-o—"

"So?" Steve O'Leary prompted, watching his chief closely.

"Maybe it's something *small* enough to have done the job. A virus, say. A complex molecule halfway between the animal and mineral kingdom, something not quite alive but a million times more dangerous than anything that is."

"But Vic, wouldn't I have hit it with the electron microscope?" Harry Lutz spread his hands nervously. "And whatever I muffed—well, the robot eye is still classifying five thousand specimens a minute. If a virus did for the birds and beasts here, we'd have come across at least one culture by now."

"Would we? If it were a virus that couldn't adapt to plant life, it might not be very active—or very numerous—at the moment. Then again if we did turn up a specimen, how would we know?"

"The robot eye—"

Vic Carlton grimaced. *"The robot eye!* One way, Lutz, not to grow old in this service is to believe everything the manuals tell you about the equipment. Sure, the robot eye attached to the electron microscope makes a fine pathologist. But all the robot eye has behind it is a robot memory—a file of every microscopic and sub-microscopic form of life which, in the parts of the galaxy explored up to this date, have been found inimical to man. If it sees something enough like one of the items in the file to close a ten-decimal relay, we're warned. And it's warned us of a dozen or so species on this planet which it turns out our stuff can handle. But there's never yet been anything like a robot imagination. Your little machine, Harry, can't scratch its mounting and say 'Now, I don't like the looks of that baby there, harmless though it may seem.' Whenever a robot eye hits something completely out of its memory file, you know what happens."

"Yeah." O'Leary chuckled and swung himself up to his bunk. "Three corpses in Scout uniforms and, after the investigative expedition, maybe another item for the eye's robot memory. That's the way we learn, Lutz, old soak: trial and error. Only, me brave young C Scout, we're the trials and—ever so often—we're the errors too." He lay back on the bunk, and, as his huge red head disappeared from view, they could hear his deep voice caroling, *"Oh, I'm the bosun tight and the midshipmite—"*

Lutz looked unhappy as the other man slid into his morbid humor. The enforced seclusion aboard the little ship, from which he could see the gloriously free miles of acreage which surrounded them, had not done Steve O'Leary any particular good. He was too long in the service to question discipline, especially as regarded safety measures; but his subconscious could whisper irritably, and rumors of fear leaped irresistibly upwards in his mind.

More than ever, Vic felt himself drawn to the younger man. At least Lutz wasn't riding a recent scare: he had no idea, as yet, how cold his back could get.

"Look," the mission commander said kindly. "I'm not saying that there is a bug out there waiting to knock us off. I don't know. Maybe out here in the Hole, there's some radiation effect which inhibits the evolution of complex animal forms. Maybe. I'm just saying that we keep looking and keep guessing until we feel we've exhausted every possibility of danger. *Then,* when we finally take a stroll outside the ship, we wear space-suits with both Grojen shielding and Mannheim baffles."

O'Leary's head came up out of his bunk again. "Hey!" he said disappointedly. "That much weight and we'll have to use electrical medullas to walk. I was looking forward to a hop, skip and jump under my own power. A little run across the ground would feel awful good."

He shut up and lay down under Vic's thoughtful glare. And it was the thought behind the glare that made Vic tell him the day they were ready to begin exploring the surface:

"I'm taking Lutz with me. We want the man in the ship to know what to do in case something pops. So you're elected, Steve."

The redhead watched them struggle into cumbersome, equipment-laden space-suits. He kneaded huge hands into his hips. "That's not customary, Vic, and you know it. Man on a bounce is the first one through the lock."

"If the commander sees it that way," he was told curtly. "I don't. You'll get your exercise later. Meanwhile, I want you to sit over those jets like a runner in a hundred-yard dash. If we get into trouble and you can help us, fine; but if it looks at all tight or too unusual, remember the primary purpose of the mission is to gather information about the Hole. So you cut and run."

O'Leary turned his back and began working the air-lock. "Thanks, pal," he muttered. "I can see myself back in Sandstorm swearing to the boys that you gave me exactly those orders. I can see myself."

They climbed down the ladder and started across the surface. Vic, in the lead, was being very cautious; behind him, Harry Lutz sweated, stumbled and cursed in the huge suit with which even a year's training had not thoroughly familiarized him.

The commander stopped in what looked like a grove of chest-high elm trees. "Take it easy, Lutz," he suggested. "You're carrying a lot of weight and you can't possibly move it all correctly. The trick in using an electrical medulla is not to let your right hand know what your left is doing. I know you had enough workouts in those things back at the academy to use the fingers on all the correct buttons. It'll be second nature if you give it a chance. Just relax and take in the scenery: concentrate on what you want to do, where you want to go—not how you want to do it. And once you stop thinking about them, your fingers will take care of the medulla-switches for you. They've been educated to do the job."

He heard the C Scout take a deep breath through the radio phones. Then, as Lutz looked about him and relaxed visibly, his pace became more regular, the movements of the suit—weighted down as it was with Grojen shielding, Mannheim baffles and intricate operating apparatus—even and controlled. Lutz had managed to shift his thoughts from the motor to the conscious level; once that was done, he could be of maximum assistance while his fingers played over the proper switches inside their enormous metal mittens.

Good kid, Vic smiled to himself. Lots of rookies flopped about for days after they had occasion to use electrical medullas on actual mission work. Lutz had enough control to overcome the inevitable panic resulting from walking on a strange world for the first time in a garment that was essentially a robot. He caught on fast. He tried hard.

*That's the way I'd like my son to—*Vic shut the thought off. There was work to do. And a younger, more inexperienced man to watch. *Still—*

They picked their way through the miniature trees, Lutz now striding along easily, and up a slight rise in the ground. They stood at the top of the small hill finally and looked around while luxurious branches waved in the direction of their stomachs.

From the stern mountains in the distance to the stream dodging shrilly about rusty old rocks nearby, the land on which they stood yawned under a summer sun. Pink and blue grasses stretched and waved at each other. Mist rolled out of the huge lake a mile or so away.

Lutz chuckled inside his helmet. "Always did want to see what a vacation paradise looked like before the real estate boys moved in!"

"If they ever do. See anything moving here right now?"

"Well, that—and these." Harry Lutz indicated the towering bramble forest to their right and the dwarf trees around them.

"Plants. Trees and bushes bending with the wind, waving with the breeze. Nothing like a rabbit, say, breaking cover as we step over his burrow, or a bee skimming along and looking for an appetizing flower. No creatures like bugs working the soil, no birds flying overhead and considering the possibilities of bug-dinners."

"But we knew that already—from the telescanner."

"I know," the mission commander scraped a metallic mitten along his helmet. "But why? The plants aren't carnivorous: with minor alterations in chemistry and morphology, you might expect to find them on Earth. I tell you I don't like it, Lutz. Why shouldn't this planet have a zoology?"

"Maybe all the animals went into the Hole," Lutz suggested brightly.

Carlton stared at him. "You know," he began, "you may really have something there. Of course, the Hole in Cygnus is an astronomical term," he went on hurriedly. "But there's a lot out here they never heard of on Mount Palomar or Sahara University either. 'Maybe all the animals went into the Hole.' What about *that*—"

"Hey, Vic!" O'Leary's voice from the ship. "Green ball—one of those spore-things—rolling straight for us."

"From where?"

"You should be able to see it in a moment. Due north of that mountain range. There! See that speck coming through those twin peaks?"

The two Scouts outside the ship unsheathed supersonics and crouched as the speck grew into a dot and then into a ball of green hurtling at an almost unbelievable speed.

"Better go back?" Lutz asked nervously.

"We'd never make it—not with that baby traveling as fast as it is. Just keep still and keep down: I've an idea that the solution—"

"More of 'em," Steve O'Leary's voice cut in excitedly. "Two bowling up in a line from the southwest. I don't think they're spores at all; I think they're intelligent and mighty like animules. And they all—Hey-y-y! I just located the mother-lode with the telescanner. Guess where?"

"Let's play games another day," Vic told him.

"From that mess of white tentacles touching the planet on the opposite side. A whole flock of green balls just boiled out. Could those tentacles be alive, have sense-organs? Doesn't seem logical, though, when you consider a couple of them are floating in empty space—"

"Forget the tentacles, O'Leary, and concentrate on the green blobs for a while. I believe we started all this excitement—Lutz and I—by walking out of the ship. Stand by the jets for a scram—with or without us."

"Not on your rating. That's final, Vic! Either you boys fight your way back in or I come out to join you."

Carlton bit his lip. The green ball was almost overhead now, its smooth, completely featureless surface flickering most oddly. That was always the trouble with a man making a bounce. He fluctuated between abysmal fright and mountainous bravado, both nothing else than a simple fear of being afraid—and both always coming up at the wrong times. Right now, he wanted a subordinate who could understand the supreme importance of the first mission to the Hole, who could appreciate a situation where information might be a thousand times more important than the lives or opinions of others—and who would be rock-steady in an emergency instead of skittering about with a private neurosis.

"All right, O'Leary. Secondary attack precautions. Get into a space-suit and man the bow gun. Robots on the others. Switch to full visiplate hook-up. But keep those jets ready to blast!"

"Uh—commander," Lutz broke in. "Three of those balls overhead. More coming. But they're ignoring us: they just bang around the ship."

Vic Carlton stared upward. He'd never seen anything quite like these spheres. Their color might argue for chlorophyl, but they were far too animate, too purposeful, to have botanical origins. Vehicles in which sat sentient organisms? That might account for the lack of such things as eyes and locomotive appendages. But, then, where was the jet-trail or any other evidence of a propulsive device? And surely the way they expanded and contracted seemed to point to an intrinsic life of their own. That was really odd, now—

"Could they be breathing?" the C Scout wondered aloud.

"No. Too irregular for respiration, I'd say. Just keep still, Lutz, and wait it out. This is the hardest part of a mission, boy, but patience has saved more lives than all the Grojen shielding ever made."

They waited, inside their great suits, while the number of balls increased to twelve, all shooting about the ship in straight, determined lines. Evidently, Vic reflected, while they sat still, they went unnoticed.

Suddenly, one of the spheres paused outside the airlock. "Seems to know its way around," O'Leary commented from the ship. He laughed twice, the second time after a few moments pause. "I'm getting jumpy, Vic."

"Don't," he was advised. "They may be smart enough to know how we enter and leave the ship, but they can't have seen many space-ships if they get this close to a fully armed one. Sit on your nerves, Steve: once they thin out and we can get back, we might try communicating with them. Although they don't seem to be responsive. You're wearing side-arms, I hope?"

"Supersonics. And a heavy blaster across my lap. Blow a hole through the hull if I use it, but if I have to—Say! Is that baby doing what I see through the visiplate?"

It was. The ball had withdrawn a little distance from the ship and came rushing towards it rapidly. It bounced gently, soundlessly, off the hull, retired and repeated the process. The horizontal lines in which it moved and the insistent nature of its repetitious approach reminded the three Scouts of a fist knocking at a door.

Then—it disappeared!

They shook their heads and grimaced at the spot where it had last been in the midst of another rush at the air-lock. It was gone, with no faintest emerald trace left behind on the lazy air. Around the ship, eleven balls shot back and forth, back and forth, in absolutely straight lines. But there had been twelve a moment ago!

"C-Commander, wh-what do you think h-happened?"

"Don't know, Lutz. But I definitely don't like it."

"Neither do I," O'Leary whispered in their radio phones.

"This is one of those moments in a B Scout's life when he wonders what he ever saw in an A Scout rating to make him leave home and mama. I'd like to be back in— *No!* Vic, It's *impossible!* It couldn't—It—"

"What happened? Steve! What's going on?"

"The damn ball materialized inside the ship—just as I was reaching over to the—not five feet from me—made a rush at my head—almost got—" Steve O'Leary's voice came over in jerky snatches as if he were spitting out each fragment between jumps. "Chasing me all over the Control Room—*no, you don't*—caroming off the bulkheads like a billiard—wait, I think I have a sight—"

A tremendous roar. O'Leary had used the blaster. Echo after echo piled crazily upon their eardrums and a jagged hole flapped open near the nose of the ship as if it had been punched out.

"Missed! Could've sworn I had a clear sight—blast went practically head-on—don't know *how* I missed— now, maybe with a supersonic—well, what would you call *that? Vic!* It's disappeared again! Clean gone! I'm getting out of here!"

"Careful, Steve!" Carlton yelled. "You're panicky!"

There was no reply. Instead, the air-lock swung open, and Steve O'Leary, space-suited to almost twice his normal size, leaped out. He carried a supersonic in his left hand and a blaster in his right and he came out shooting. Eleven green balls converged on him, riding imperturbably through his blasts.

The two Scouts on the hill had leaped to their feet. They shot bolt after bolt of high frequency sound, sound which could dissolve any conceivable organic structure into its component chemicals. They might have been using water-pistols for all the effect they had.

A twelfth ball appeared directly in O'Leary's path. It began the size of an apple, and, almost before their eyes could register the change, had coruscated glaucously to the diameter of a life boat. A little in advance of its fellows, it shot at the B Scout.

It touched him.

And he screamed.

His scream seemed to have begun years ago and continue into the unguessable future. And then, the entire space-suit seemed to fly open and—not O'Leary, but his insides came out. Where a metallic figure had been running, covered with a Grojen shield and lightly draped with Mannheim baffles, there was now only stomach and spleen, liver and intestine, stretched fantastically, unbelievably, into the shape of Steve O'Leary. The figure took another step, and the scream ululated out of human recognition. Then it stopped.

O'Leary was gone. And the green ball was gone.

The other balls had passed over the spot where Steve O'Leary had disappeared. Two of them disappeared in turn. Nine returned to the ship and continued their determined, whipping investigation.

Lutz was being violently sick inside his space-suit. Vic fought for self-control. *Had he or had he not seen the emerald ball change to a deep olive and then to the color of pouring blood just before it went out?*

"Listen, kid," he said rapidly. "Keep still, keep absolutely, perfectly still—no matter what happens. Don't even roll your eyes. I think I know what those things are, and I don't think anything we have can stop them. Our only hope is to avoid attracting attention. So don't move until I give you the word. Got that?"

He heard Lutz's breathing become more regular. "Y-yes, commander. But don't they remember us shooting at them? And can't they see us standing here in plain sight?"

"Not if they're what I suspect. Relax, kid, relax as far back as you can. Remember, not a movement of any kind you can control. And no conversation for a while. Nothing. Just watch and wait."

They waited. They watched. They waited for hours, half-reclining in their immobile suits, while the green balls tore back and forth, appeared and disappeared silently, steadily, with unwavering purpose. They watched the blue line running the length of their precious ship—the line that proclaimed it a Scout vessel and able to outrun anything in space—they watched the blue line dissolve into the gray metal around it under the thick suds of twilight. And they made no movement, no, not even when a bloated sphere of green expanded in front of them suddenly and seemed to consider them under invisible optic organs before losing interest and scudding away.

That was the hardest part, after all, Vic decided: not moving even though the feeling that they were under surveillance increased with every second; not jerking suddenly, though most ancient instincts shouted that it was time to run, that this very moment they would be attacked by the unseeable.

He came to appreciate his companion's qualities in the course of the awful vigil: not many men could maintain that necessary exterior calm on the very knife-edge of extinction. *One good kid.*

They waited; they watched; they didn't move. And they thought about Steve O'Leary. . . .

Finally, two of the balls rose and flew off to the north. An hour later, two more followed. The remaining five came to rest above the ship, forming the points of a rough pentagon.

"All right, Lutz," the A Scout murmured. "We can unbend—just a little! Six hours of daylight. We'll sleep two hours apiece, you first, one watching while the other takes a nap. That'll give us some rest before we make our play; and maybe in that time the five tumblebugs will decide to go home."

"What are they, commander? What in the name of intergalactic space can they be?"

"What are they? A leak in the Hole of Cygnus. They're where all the animals went."

"I—I don't understand."

Carlton almost gestured impatiently, stopped himself just in time. "There's much that's peculiar about the Hole. Not merely the absence of ordinary celestial phenomena, the rarity of stars and such-like, but loopholes in natural law which you find nowhere else. A minority of modern theories consider this general area the starting-place of our particular universe; whether they begin with space warping in on itself because it got tired of standing around in time, or with one version or another of the explosion of a primordial atom—whatever they begin with these days, they work in the Hole in Cygnus somehow as the place where it might have occurred."

"Yes. Ever since Boker came out here two hundred years ago and discovered the sectors of chronological gap."

"Right, kid. Now I don't claim to know how the universe started. But I'm willing to bet my next meal in Sandstorm against the dust on your right boot that this was where it did. And from the looks of things, the area around Cygnus never recovered. It remained a hole in space where all kinds of stuff that shouldn't be, is—and vice versa. That moment or millennium of creation tore it up plenty. And among the tears, among the cuts that were never healed, I classify those white tentacle thingumabobs all over this system."

"And the green balls came through the one on this planet from—from—"

"From some place outside. From another universe which we can't reach or even imagine."

Lutz thought about that for a moment. "On another plane, you mean, commander?"

"On another dimension. The fourth, to be specific."

"But 'way back in the twentieth century they proved

that the fourth dimension was time and *we* move through it!"

"I mean a fourth spatial dimension, Lutz. A universe where there's length, breadth, height—and, well, one *more* direction, besides. Time, too, but even a conceivable two-dimensional creature must have duration in order to exist. And that's the way to understand those babies: what they can do, what they can't, what happened to O'Leary and what hope we have of covering those sixty yards to the ship and taking off. Analogy. Think of a two-dimensional man."

"You mean width and length, but no height? Gee—I don't know. I guess we'd see his skin as a thin line around his skeleton and internal organs. And—wait a minute—he'd be able to move and see only on an absolutely flat surface!"

Carlton silently thanked the academy officials for entrance examination that weeded out the least imaginative. "You're doing fine. Now suppose we stuck a finger into this two-dimensional world. The man in it would see the finger as a circle—just as we see these creatures as spheres. When the tip had gone through his world and the finger proper was visible, he would feel the circle had grown larger; when we pulled the finger out, he'd say it had disappeared. If we wanted to eat him, say, we could hover above him while he ran from the place where he'd last seen us. Then pounce down in front of him, and he'd think we'd suddenly materialized out of thin air. And, if we wanted to lift him into our world, our space—"

"We'd pick him up by the skin and his insides would momentarily be the only part of him visible in his world." Lutz shivered involuntarily. "Ugh. Then those balls are sections of fourth-dimensional fingers—or pseudopods?"

"I don't know. I suspect, though, that these creatures are only fourth-dimensional equivalents of our very simple forms—anything from bacteria to worms—but still dangerous as death itself. I don't think they're very complicated animals on their world because they seem to have pretty elementary sense-perceptions. They don't hear us, smell us or feel us; and they only chase us when we move. That all adds up to a fairly primitive organism, even in four dimensions. It would explain why there's no animal life on this planet, but plants of almost every kind: animals are motile, so they were chased and eaten; plants generally grow in one spot, so they were ignored."

"But, Vic, we have to move to get back in the ship!"

"We have to move, but not in straight lines. Not the way those balls move back and forth, not the way O'Leary moved. We'll run a purposely erratic course to the airlock, we'll stop unexpectedly, we'll zigzag, we'll turn around and double on our tracks. It'll take up extra time, but I'm betting that our green chums haven't the sensory or mental equipment to solve a random movement fast enough."

"Poor O'Leary! It'll seem all wrong going back without that big loud redhead."

"We aren't going, kid, until we get inside that ship and flush those jets behind us. Now grab some sleep before we run out of night."

As the C Scout closed his eyes obediently, Carlton risked a glance at him. Tired, scared as hell, but still swallowing orders with alacrity, still willing to take chances. *One good kid,* he repeated to himself. *Wonder if he's started shaving yet. Nope—with that jet-black hair and creamy complexion a beard would be very obvious, even a couple of hours growth.*

Wonder who he has waiting for him back home. Probably only his mother; doesn't act like the kind of kid who's played around much with girls. Probably only the girl, the one he took to the graduation ball at the academy.

Wonder what Kay would think of Lutz—would she understand him?

Wonder who's waiting for O'Leary. . . .

The green spheres above the ship were perfectly still, their smooth bodies ignoring even the stern night wind that roared down from the mountains. Asleep, in their own peculiar way? Or waiting?

Lutz and O'Leary: two good guys, Kay. Adolescents? Spacewash!

Vic let Lutz sleep for almost three hours before awakening him. It would take two to do this job right, and he wanted the younger man's nerves to settle as much as possible.

"I lost track of *my* nerves about five years ago off Sirius," he explained.

"All the same, Vic, all the same, you can't punish yourself like that! Why you won't even have a full hour yourself."

"It'll do me fine. Now just stand guard and whistle once—loudly—if anything is on the verge of popping. And whistle at the end of the hour."

He fell asleep instantly and dreamlessly with the ease of the experienced Scout who has used his space-suit as a flophouse many times. He woke a moment before the hour was up, when the alarm clock buried in his subconscious went off.

Lutz was singing under his breath to keep himself company. Almost without sound, just enough of the words came through over the radio phones to make the song clear. Carlton listened to Lutz sing with all the loneliness, the longing, of the last man alive:

> . . . and end my days
> On some mould'ring ball.
> No more to the stars will I go—
> O lads!
> No more to the stars will I go!

"First," the commander broke in cheerfully, "you need a maiden's praise, kid. To hold you in thrall. But you wouldn't understand that part."

"Sorry I woke you, Vic. I was just going to whistle. And when it comes to a maiden's praise, I do as well as the next guy. Had a tough time getting away for this mission, let me tell you!"

"Who—your sister? Or the girl next door?" This light banter would develop just the right mood for what they had to do.

"My *sister!*" Lutz laughed boyishly. "Hell, no. My wife."

Carlton was amazed. "Are *you* married?"

"Married? I sincerely hope for the sake of my children that I am!"

"Well, I'll be—How many do you have?"

"Two. Two girls. The youngest, Jeanette, is only three months old. She's a blonde, like her mother."

"Yes," Vic mused. "Kay's a blonde. Her daughter would probably—"

"Kay? Your wife, commander?"

"No. My fiancée," Vic told him stiffly. "Well, one good thing about marriage, Lutz; your dependents are well taken care of. The Scout finance department doesn't recognize engagement rings. I guess that's a comfort to a husband and father if he's knocked off somewhere in emptiness."

The C Scout looked down at the ship. "All five of them still there, commander. I'm ready to go any time you give the word."

There was a pause. "Look, Lutz," Carlton began awkwardly. "I'm sorry if—if—"

"No offense taken if none's given, Vic. Only thing, way back in my second year at the academy I decided that I wanted to get married, I wanted to have a family—*and* I wanted to be a Scout. All three. So you figure it out. Me, I find it hurts my head."

"All right, then; let's concentrate on what we have to do. When I yell, we leap sideways and come down upon the ship in two converging arcs. Using medulla-switches, we can run twice as fast as a horse. We don't run more than two steps in a straight line if we can remember it—and we've got to remember it! First man in kicks the jets over. If the other man isn't in by the time the ship takes off, he's left behind. No second chance, no waiting a moment longer, no looking back. I think if we do this right, we can confuse them enough to get away together, but if we don't—remember that we can't help each other and that our records and interpretation *must* make it to Sandstorm: Check?"

"Check. And good luck, Vic."

"Good luck, Harry. And good running."

The A Scout looked around one last time to judge the ground he would have to travel. His fingers crept over the switches in the mittens, ready to galvanize the suit into a breakneck speed. "Now!" he roared, leaping off to the left.

As he pounded down the slope, his speed and weight uprooting the tiny trees in his twisting path, he could see Lutz, far off to his right, zigzagging with him. They might make it. They might—

They got to twenty yards of the ship before the green balls noticed them. And streaked straight for them without hesitation.

Carlton stopped, leaped backward, sideward and came around the stern of the ship in a great curve. Lutz was coming down the other side, his course resembling a drunk with rocket attachment. The air-lock gaped open between them. Immense balls sped by hungrily, almost touching, almost— Only eleven yards. Double back and leap forward again. Nine yards. Jump away from the ship and cut in at a sharp angle. Seven.

"Look, commander, I'm in—I made it!" Only six yards from the air-lock—only eighteen feet! Harry Lutz lost his head. He came up in a tremendous broad-jump powered by the motor of the heavy suit. He aimed at the open door of the air-lock, evidently intending to catch it in mid-air and pull himself inside. But it was he who was caught in mid-air.

A green sphere materialized twelve feet from the lock and Lutz, unable to check himself, smashed into it. Almost before he began screaming, almost before he began to turn inside out, the remaining four balls had shot to the other side of the lock to observe or partake of the prey.

The way was clear for Carlton. He leaped inside, almost brushing the crimsoning ball—wondering whether he could have done it if they hadn't caught Harry Lutz.

"Poor little Jeanette," he wept as Lutz's scream bit and clawed at his ear-drums, "poor kid, she's only three months old!" he cried as he pulled the red switch on the control panel and jumped away for a moment just in case. "Poor little blonde Jeanette, she's only a baby! She can't remember anything," he screamed in sympathy to Lutz's continuing scream as he swung balance-control, adjusted acceleration-helix, felt the ship whip up and outward with him—and continued to zigzag about the control room because you never knew, you just never knew about those green balls.

But when he had switched to interstellar shoot, and found Lutz's scream still in his ears, still rising in insane volume, when he found himself unable to stop leaping backward, forward, sideward, about the control room—he attached the main oxygen tanks to his helmet and turned on the automatic alarm.

A patrol ship got to him three days later. There was no air in the little vessel because, while the lock had closed automatically upon takeoff, the hole in the nose had never been repaired. But Vic Carlton, completely exhausted and with eyes like diseased tomatoes, was alive in a space-suit designed to *keep* a man alive under the most incredible conditions. He had disconnected his helmet phones and, when they hauled him out of his ship, he kept beating both mittened hands against his head in the region of his ears.

They gave him an anaesthetic in the patrol ship hospital and set a fast course for Sol.

"Poor little Jeanette Lutz," he whispered painfully just before he fell asleep. "She's only three months old."

"Are you sure you can pull him through?" a perspiring commissioner asked in the hospital on Ganymede. "Because if there's any danger that you can't, let's use a hypnotic probe. The information he's carrying is worth the risk of permanent damage to his mind."

"We'll pull him through," the doctor said, making unhappy early-morning grimaces as he washed his mouth with his tongue. "We'll pull him through all right. According to his charts, he's survived concentrated therapy before. No point in blowing out his brains with a probe when he'll be able to tell you everything you want to know in a week or two."

"I told them everything," Vic informed Kay three weeks later when he met her on the main floor of the Scout Operations Building. "I told them off, too. How can you expect a man to take a bounce, I said, when the Service itself won't? That's what the Patrol big-brains decided—that the Hole is still too dangerous for anything mankind has. They're going to wait a while before sending another exploring party there. *Well,* I said—"

He stopped as the elevator doors slid open and the crowd of Scouts surrounding the three helmeted ones in the center moved toward the double doors chattering and chafing. .

"Look at Spinelli, fellows! He's dead already!"

"Poor Spinelli, his first command! Hey, Spin, this is the bounce Carlton wouldn't take! He musta known something!"

"Hey, Tronck! What're you looking so green about!"

"Steady there, Spinelli. You're a commander now!"

Vic's hand crept to his chest as the men passed. He fingered the gold star which glowed from the spot where, an hour before, a silver rocket had poised.

Kay touched the star, too. Her back was to the men marching to the ship, but her eyes shone into Vic's. "Commissioner Carlton! It sounds as if it was always meant to be just that. Alliterative, too! Oh, Vic, this is the way we said it would be—this is the way we both wanted it. You, with the fire still in you, knowing that you're a grown man, knowing what you want—"

From the distance, they could hear the song:

> If it's a girl, dress her up in lace;
> If it's a boy, send the bastard off to space.

"Darling," she whispered, pressing his hand against her cheek. "We'll have lots of lace *and* lots of space. We'll have everything."

Vic didn't answer. He stood, ignoring her completely, as the three men sang themselves into the slender little ship with the long blue stripe. When the ground crew scattered with warning yells of "Jets away! Jets away away, jets away!" he took one resolute step forward, stopped—and put his hands in his pockets.

Then the sudden scream and clatter of flame, dying almost before it had been felt; then the silver pencil up in the sky that left a thin line of brightest scarlet behind it. The ship was gone, and a cloud waddled over its trail, but still Vic stared upward. Kay said nothing.

When, at last, he turned back to her, his eyes were full of middle age.

■ SHE ONLY GOES OUT,
AT NIGHT . . . ■

IN THIS part of the country, folks think that Doc Judd carries magic in his black leather satchel. He's *that* good.

Ever since I lost my leg in the sawmill, I've been all-around handyman at the Judd place. Lots of times when Doc gets a night call after a real hard day, he's too tired to drive, so he hunts me up and I become a chauffeur too. With the shiny plastic leg that Doc got me at a discount, I can stamp the gas pedal with the best of them.

We roar up to the farmhouse and, while Doc goes inside to deliver a baby or swab grandma's throat, I sit in the car and listen to them talk about what a ball of fire the old Doc is. In Groppa County, they'll tell you Doc Judd can handle *anything*. And I nod and listen, nod and listen.

But all the time I'm wondering what they'd think of the way he handled his only son falling in love with a vampire. . . .

It was a terrifically hot summer when Steve came home on vacation—real blister weather. He wanted to drive his father around and kind of help with the chores, but Doc said that after the first tough year of medical school anyone deserved a vacation.

"Summer's a pretty quiet time in our line," he told the

boy. "Nothing but poison ivy and such until we hit the polio season in August. Besides, you wouldn't want to shove old Tom out of his job, would you? No, Stevie, you just bounce around the countryside in your jalopy and enjoy yourself."

Steve nodded and took off. And I mean took off. About a week later, he started coming home five or six o'clock in the morning. He'd sleep till about three in the afternoon, lazy around for a couple of hours and, come eight-thirty, off he'd rattle in his little hot-rod. Road-houses, we figured, or maybe some girl . . .

Doc didn't like it, but he'd brought up the boy with a nice easy hand and he didn't feel like saying anything just yet. Old buttinsky Tom, though— I was different. I'd helped raise the kid since his mother died, and I'd walloped him when I caught him raiding the ice-box.

So I dropped a hint now and then, kind of asking him, like, not to go too far off the deep end. I could have been talking to a stone fence for all the good it did. Not that Steve was rude. He was just too far gone in whatever it was to pay attention to me.

And then the other stuff started and Doc and I forgot about Steve.

Some kind of weird epidemic hit the kids of Groppa County and knocked twenty, thirty, of them flat on their backs.

"It's almost got me beat, Tom," Doc would confide in me as we bump-bump-bumped over dirty back-country roads. "It acts like a bad fever, yet the rise in temperature is hardly noticeable. But the kids get very weak and their blood count goes way down. And it stays that way, no matter what I do. Only good thing, it doesn't seem to be fatal—so far."

Every time he talked about it, I felt a funny twinge in my stump where it was attached to the plastic leg. I got so uncomfortable that I tried to change the subject, but that didn't go with Doc. He'd gotten used to thinking out his problems by talking to me, and this epidemic thing was pretty heavy on his mind.

He'd written to a couple of universities for advice, but they didn't seen to be of much help. And all the time, the parents of the kids stood around waiting for him to pull a cellophane-wrapped miracle out of his little black bag, because, as they said in Groppa County, there was nothing could go wrong with a human body that Doc Judd couldn't take care of some way or other. And all the time, the kids got weaker and weaker.

Doc got big, bleary bags under his eyes from sitting up nights going over the latest books and medical magazines he'd ordered from the city. Near as I could tell he'd find nothing, even though lots of times he'd get to bed almost as late as Steve.

And then he brought home the handkerchief. Soon as I saw it, my stump gave a good, hard, extra twinge and I wanted to walk out of the kitchen. Tiny, fancy handkerchief, it was, all embroidered linen and lace edges.

"What do you think, Tom? Found this on the floor of the bedroom of the Stopes' kids. Neither Betty nor Willy have any idea where it came from. For a bit, I thought I might have a way of tracing the source of infection, but those kids wouldn't lie. If they say they never saw it before, then that's the way it is." He dropped the handkerchief on the kitchen table that I was clearing up, stood there sighing. "Betty's anemia is beginning to look serious. I wish I knew . . . I wish . . . Oh, well." He walked out to the study, his shoulders bent like they were under a sack of cement.

I was still staring at the handkerchief, chewing on a fingernail, when Steve bounced in. He poured himself a cup of coffee, plumped it down on the table and saw the handkerchief.

"Hey," he said. "That's Tatiana's. How did it get here?"

I swallowed what was left of the fingernail and sat down very carefully opposite him. "Steve," I asked, and then stopped because I had to massage my aching stump. "Stevie, you know a girl who owns that handkerchief? A girl named Tatiana?"

"Sure. Tatiana Latianu. See, there are her initials embroidered in the corner—T. L. She's descended from the Rumanian nobility; family goes back about five hundred years. I'm going to marry her."

"She the girl you've been seeing every night for the past month?"

He nodded. "She only goes out at night. Hates the glare of the sun. You know, poetic kind of girl. And Tom, she's so *beautiful*. . . ."

For the next hour, I just sat there and listened to him. And I felt sicker and sicker. Because I'm Rumanian myself, on my mother's side. And I knew why I'd been getting those twinges in my stump.

She lived in Brasket Township, about twelve miles away. Tom had run into her late one night on the road when her convertible had broken down. He'd given her a lift to her house—she'd just rented the old Mead Mansion—and he'd fallen for her, hook, line and whole darn fishing rod.

Lots of times, when he arrived for a date, she'd be out, driving around the countryside in the cool night air, and he'd have to play cribbage with her maid, an old beak-faced Rumanian biddy, until she got back. Once or twice, he'd tried to go after her in his hot-rod, but that had led to trouble. When she wanted to be alone, she had told him, she wanted to be *alone*. So that was that. He waited for her night after night. But when she got back, according to Steve, she really made up for everything. They listened to music and talked and danced and ate strange Rumanian dishes that the maid whipped up. Until dawn. Then he came home.

Steve put his hand on my arm. "Tom, you know that poem—*The Owl and the Pussy-Cat?* I've always thought the last line was beautiful. 'They danced by the light of the moon, the moon, they danced by the light of the moon.' That's what my life will be like with Tatiana. If only she'll have me. I'm still having trouble talking her into it."

I let out a long breath. "The first good thing I've heard," I said without thinking. "Marriage to *that* girl—"

When I saw Steve's eyes, I broke off. But it was too late.

"What the hell do you mean, Tom: *that* girl? You've never even met her."

I tried to twist out of it, but Steve wouldn't let me. He was real sore. So I figured the best thing was to tell him the truth.

"Stevie. Listen. Don't laugh. Your girl friend is a vampire."

He opened his mouth slowly. "Tom, you're off your—

"No, I'm not." And I told him about vampires. What I'd heard from my mother who'd come over from the old country, from Transylvania, when she was twenty. How they can live and have all sorts of strange powers—just so long as they have a feast of human blood once in a while. How the vampire taint is inherited, usually just one child in the family getting it. And how they go out only at night, because sunlight is one of the things that can destroy them.

Steve turned pale at this point. But I went on. I told him about the mysterious epidemic that had hit the kids of Groppa County—and made them anemic. I told him about his father finding the handkerchief in the Stopes' house, near two of the sickest kids. And I told him—but all of a sudden I was talking to myself. Steve tore out of the kitchen. A second or two later, he was off in the hot-rod.

He came back about eleven-thirty, looking as old as his father. I was right, all right. When he'd wakened Tatiana and asked her straight, she'd broken down and wept a couple of buckets-full. Yes, she was a vampire, but she'd only got the urge a couple of months ago. She'd fought it until her mind began to break when the craving hit her. She'd only touched kids, because she was afraid of grown-ups—they might wake up and be able to catch her. But she'd kind of worked on a lot of kids at one time, so that no one kid would lose too much blood. Only the craving had been getting stronger. . . .

And still Steve had asked her to marry him! "There must be a way of curing it," he said. "It's a sickness like any other sickness." But she, and—believe me—I thanked God, had said no. She'd pushed him out and made him leave. "Where's Dad?" he asked. "He might know."

I told him that his father must have left at the same time he did, and hadn't come back yet. So the two of us sat and thought. *And thought.*

When the telephone rang, we both almost fell out of our seats. Steve answered it, and I heard him yelling into the mouthpiece.

He ran into the kitchen, grabbed me by the arm and hauled me out into his hot-rod. "That was Tatiana's maid, Magda," he told me as we went blasting down the highway. "She says Tatiana got hysterical after I left, and a few minutes ago she drove away in her convertible. She wouldn't say where she was going. Magda says she thinks Tatiana is going to do away with herself."

"*Suicide?* But if she's a vampire, how—" And all of a sudden I knew just how. I looked at my watch. "Stevie," I said, "drive to Crispin Junction. And drive like holy hell!"

He opened that hot-rod all the way. It looked as if the

motor was going to tear itself right off the car. I remember
we went around curves just barely touching the road with
the rim of one tire.

We saw the convertible as soon as we entered Crispin
Junction. It was parked by the side of one of the three
roads that cross the town. There was a tiny figure in a
flimsy nightdress standing in the middle of the deserted
street. My leg stump felt like it was being hit with a
hammer.

The church clock started to toll midnight just as we
reached her. Steve leaped out and knocked the pointed
piece of wood out of her hands. He pulled her into his
arms and let her cry.

I was feeling pretty bad at this point. Because all I'd
been thinking of was how Steve was in love with a vampire. I hadn't looked at it from her side. She'd been
enough in love with him to try to kill herself the *only* way
a vampire could be killed—by driving a stake through her
heart on a crossroads at midnight.

And she was a pretty little creature. I'd pictured one of
these siren dames: you know, tall, slinky, with a tight
dress. A witch. But this was a very frightened, very upset
young lady who got in the car and cuddled up in Steve's
free arm like she'd taken a lease on it. And I could tell she
was even younger than Steve.

So, all the time we were driving back, I was thinking to
myself *these kids have got plenty trouble.* Bad enough to
be in love with a vampire, but to be a vampire in love
with a normal human being . . .

"But how *can* I marry you?" Tatiana wailed. "What
kind of home life would we have? And Steve, one night I
might even get hungry enough to attack *you!*"

The only thing none of us counted on was Doc. Not
enough, that is.

Once he'd been introduced to Tatiana and heard her
story, his shoulders straightened and the lights came back

on in his eyes. The sick children would be all right now. That was most important. And as for Tatiana—

"Nonsense," he told her. "Vampirism might have been an incurable disease in the fifteenth century, but I'm sure it can be handled in the twentieth. First, this nocturnal living points to a possible allergy involving sunlight and perhaps a touch of photophobia. You'll wear tinted glasses for a bit, my girl, and we'll see what we can do with hormone injections. The need for consuming blood, however, presents a somewhat greater problem."

But he solved it.

They make blood in a dehydrated, crystalline form these days. So every night before Mrs. Steven Judd goes to sleep, she shakes some powder into a tall glass of water, drops in an ice cube or two and has her daily blood toddy. Far as I know, she and her husband are living happily ever after.

MY MOTHER WAS A WITCH

I SPENT most of my boyhood utterly convinced that my mother was a witch. No psychological trauma was involved; instead, this belief made me feel like a thoroughly loved and protected child.

My memory begins in the ragged worst of Brooklyn's Brownsville—also known as East New York—where I was surrounded by witches. Every adult woman I knew was one. Shawled conventions of them buzzed and glowered constantly at our games from nearby "stoops." Whenever my playmates swirled too boisterously close, the air turned black with angry magic: immense and complicated curses were thrown.

"May you never live to grow up," was one of the simpler, cheerier incantations. "But if you do grow up, may it be like a radish, with your head in the ground and your feet in the air." Another went: "May you itch from head to foot with scabs that drive you crazy—but only after your fingernails have broken off so you can't scratch."

These remarks were not directed at me; my mother's counter-magic was too widely feared, and I myself had been schooled in every block and parry applicable to little boys. At bedtime, my mother spat thrice, forcing the Powers with whom she was in constant familiar correspondence to reverse curses aimed at me that day back on their authors' heads three-fold, as many times as she had spit.

A witch in the family was indeed a rod and a staff of comfort.

My mother was a Yiddish witch, conducting her operations in that compote of German, Hebrew, and Slavic. This was a serious handicap: she had been born a Jewish cockney and spoke little Yiddish until she met my father, an ex-rabbinical student and fervent Socialist from Lithuania. Having bagged him in London's East End on his way to America, she set herself with immediate, wifely devotion to unlearn her useless English in place of what seemed to be the prevailing tongue of the New World.

While my father trained her to speak Yiddish fluently, he cannot have been of much help to her and their first-born in that superstitious Brooklyn slum. He held science and sweet reason to be the hope of the world; her casual, workaday necromancy horrified him. Nary a spell would he teach her: idioms, literary phrases and fine Yiddish poetry, by all means, but no spells, absolutely no spells.

She needed them. A small boy, she noted, was a prime target for malice and envy, and her new neighbors had at their disposal whole libraries of protective cantrips. Cantrips, at first, had she none. Her rank on the block was determined by the potency of her invocations and her ability—when invoked upon—to knock aside or deftly neutralize. But she sorely lacked a cursing tradition passed for generations from mother to daughter; she alone had brought no such village lore to the United States wrapped in the thick bedspreads and sewed into goosedown-stuffed pillows. My mother's only weapons were imagination and ingenuity.

Fortunately her imagination and ingenuity never failed her—once she had gotten the hang of the thing. She was a

quick study too, learning instruments of the occult as fast
as she saw them used.

"Mach a feig!" she would whisper in the grocer's as a
beaming housewife commented on my health and good
looks. Up came my fist, thumb protruding between forefinger and middle-finger in the ancient male gesture against
the female evil eye. *Feigs* were my reserve equipment
when alone: I could make them at any cursers and continue playing in the serene confidence that all unpleasant
wishes had been safely pasteurized. If an errand took me
past threatening witch faces in tenement doorways, I shot
feigs left and right, all the way down the street.

Still, my mother's best would hardly have been worth
its weight in used pentagrams if she had not stood up
worthily to Old Mrs. *Mokkeh. Mokkeh* was the lady's
nickname (it is Yiddish for plague or pestilence) and
suggested the blood-chilling imprecations she could toss
off with spectacular fluency.

This woman made such an impression on me that I
have never been able to read any of the fiercer fairy tales
without thinking of her. A tiny, square female with four
daughters, each as ugly and short as she, Mrs. *Mokkeh*
walked as if every firmly planted step left desolated terri-
tory forever and contemptuously behind. The hairy wart
on the right side of her nose was so large that behind her
back—only behind her back; who knew what she'd wish
on you if she heard you?—people giggled and said, "Her
nose has a nose."

But that was humor's limit; everything else was sheer
fright. She would squint at you, squeezing first one eye
shut, then the other, her nose wart vibrating as she rooted
about in her soul for an appropriately crippling curse. If
you were sensible, you scuttled away before the plague
that might darken your future could be fully fashioned
and slung. Not only children ran, but brave and learned
witches.

Old Mrs. *Mokkeh* was a kind of witch-in-chief. She knew curses and spells that went back to antiquity, to the crumbled ghettoes of Babylon and Thebes, and she reconstructed them in the most novel and terrible forms.

When we moved into the apartment directly above her, my mother tried hard to avoid a clash. Balls must not be bounced in the kitchen; indoor running and jumping were strictly prohibited. My mother was still learning her trade at this time and had to be cautious. She would frequently scowl at the floor and bite her lips worriedly. "The *mokkehs* that woman can think up!" she would say.

There came a day when the two of us prepared to visit cousins in the farthest arctic regions of the Bronx. Washed and scrubbed until my skin smarted all over, I was dressed in the good blue serge suit bought for the High Holy Days recently celebrated. My feet were shod in glossy black leather, my neck encircled by a white collar that had been ultimately alloyed with starch. Under this collar ran a tie of brightest red, the intense shade our neighborhood favored for burning the sensitive retina of the Evil Eye.

As we emerged from the building entrance upon the stone stoop, Mrs. *Mokkeh* and her eldest, ugliest daughter, Pearl, began climbing it from the bottom. We passed them and stopped in a knot of women chatting on the sidewalk. While my mother sought advice from her friends on express stops and train changes, I sniffed like a fretful puppy at the bulging market bags of heavy oilcloth hanging from their wrists. There was onion reek, and garlic, and the fresh miscellany of "soup greens."

The casual, barely noticing glances I drew did not surprise me; a prolonged stare at someone's well-turned-out child invited rapid and murderous retaliation. Staring was like complimenting—it only attracted the attention of the Angel of Death to a choice specimen.

I grew bored; I yawned and wriggled in my mother's

grasp. Twisting around, I beheld the witch-in-chief examining me squintily from the top of the stoop. She smiled a rare and awesomely gentle smile.

"That little boy, Pearlie," she muttered to her daughter. "A darling, a sweet one, a golden one. How nice he looks!"

My mother heard her and stiffened, but she failed to whirl, as everyone expected and deliver a brutal riposte. She had no desire to tangle with Mrs. *Mokkeh*. Our whole group listened anxiously for the Yiddish phrase customarily added to such a compliment if good will had been at all behind it—*a leben uff em,* a long life upon him.

Once it was apparent that no such qualifying phrase was forthcoming, I showed I had been well-educated. I pointed my free right hand in a spell-nullifying *feig* at my admirer.

Old Mrs. *Mokkeh* studied the *feig* with her narrow little eyes. "May that hand drop off," she intoned in the same warm, low voice. "May the fingers rot one by one and wither to the wrist. May the hand drop off, but the rot remain. May you wither to the elbow and then to the shoulder. May the whole arm rot with which you made a *feig* at me, and may it fall off and lie festering at your feet, so you will remember for the rest of your life not to make a *feig* at me."

Every woman within range of her lilting Yiddish malediction gasped and gave a mighty head-shake. Then stepping back, they cleared a space in the center of which my mother stood alone.

She turned slowly to face Old Mrs. *Mokkeh*. "Aren't you ashamed of yourself?" she pleaded. "He's only a little boy—not even five years old. Take it back."

Mrs. *Mokkeh* spat calmly on the stoop. "May it happen ten times over. Ten and twenty and a hundred times over. May he wither, may he rot. His arms, his legs, his lungs, his belly. May he vomit green gall and no doctor should be able to save him."

This was battle irrevocably joined. My mother dropped her eyes, estimating the resources of her arsenal. She must have found them painfully slender against such an opponent.

When she raised her eyes again, the women waiting for action leaned forward. My mother was known to be clever and had many well-wishers, but her youth made her a welterweight or at most a lightweight. Mrs. *Mokkeh* was an experienced heavy, a pro who had trained in the old country under famous champions. If these women had been in the habit of making book, the consensus would have been: even money she lasts one or two rounds; five to three she doesn't go the distance.

"Your daughter, Pearlie—" my mother began at last.

"Oh, momma, no!" shrieked the girl, suddenly dragged from non-combatant status into the very eye of the fight.

"Shush! Be calm," her mother commanded. After all, only green campaigners expected a frontal attack. My mother had been hit on her vulnerable flank—me—and was replying in kind. Pearl whimpered and stamped her feet, but her elders ignored this: matters of high professional moment were claiming their attention.

"Your daughter, Pearlie," the chant developed. "Now she is fourteen—may she live to a hundred and fourteen! May she marry in five years a wonderful man, a brilliant man, a doctor, a lawyer, a dentist, who will wait on her hand and foot and give her everything her heart desires."

There was a stir of tremendous interest as the kind of curse my mother was kneading became recognizable. It is one of the most difficult forms in the entire Yiddish thaumaturgical repertoire, building the subject up and up and up and ending with an annihilating crash. A well-known buildup curse goes, "May you have a bank account in every bank, and a fortune in each bank account, and may you spend every penny of it going from doctor to doctor, and no doctor should know what's the matter with you." Or: "May you own a hundred mansions, and in each mansion a hundred richly furnished bedrooms, and may you spend your life tossing from bed to bed, unable to get a single night's sleep on one of them."

To reach a peak and then explode it into an avalanche—that is the buildup curse. It requires perfect detail and even more perfect timing.

"May you give your daughter Pearlie a wedding to this wonderful husband of hers, such a wedding that the whole world will talk about it for years." Pearlie's head began a slow submergence into the collar of her dress. Her mother grunted like a boxer who has been jabbed lightly and is now dancing away.

"This wedding, may it be in all the papers, may they write about it even in books, and may you enjoy yourself at it like never before in your whole life. And one year later, may Pearlie, Pearlie and her wonderful, her rich, her considerate husband—may they present you with your first grandchild. And, *masel tov,* may it be a boy."

Old Mrs. *Mokkeh* shook unbelievingly and came down a step, her nose wart twitching and sensitive as an insect's antenna.

"And this baby boy," my mother sang, pausing to kiss her fingers before extending them to Mrs. *Mokkeh,* "what a glorious child may he be! Glorious? No. Magnificent! Such a wonderful baby boy no one will ever have seen before. The greatest rabbis coming from all over the world only to look upon him at the *bris,* so they'll be able to say in later years they were among those present at his circumcision ceremony eight days after birth. So beautiful and clever he'll be that people will expect him to say the prayers at his own *bris.* And this magnificent first grandson of yours, just one day afterward, when you are gathering happiness on every side, may he suddenly, in the middle of the night—"

"Hold!" Mrs. *Mokkeh* screamed, raising both her hands. "Stop!"

My mother took a deep breath. "And why should I stop?"

"Because I take it back! What I wished on the boy, let it be on my own head, everything I wished on him. Does that satisfy you?"

"That satisfies me," my mother said. Then she pulled my left arm up and began dragging me down the street. She walked proudly, no longer a junior among seniors, but a full and accredited sorceress.

■ **THE JESTER** ■

HISTORY CAN be as dangerous as a traffic accident: it can happen to people. And cause even more damage. One fine day—about the year 2208, say—a bright, cheerful and maybe too-smart-for-his-own-good young man wakes up to find he's tripped over his cleverest idea and crashed into a brand new age.

Away back when—early in the nineteen hundreds—people began listening to record players instead of trudging off to a vaudeville theater through the cold and wet. Later, in the radio era, most top-level executives were finding dictaphones more efficient than human stenographers and mechanical sorters better than an army of file clerks. And, at the peak of the television boom, every bride dreamed of owning a vocalex kitchen someday that would exactly obey her most casual command to heat a roast for such and such a time and baste it at such and such intervals.

With the deluxe models, of course, came a set of flavor-fix rheostats which, among other talents, could mix salads according to the recipe of a famous chef slightly better than the chef could himself. Then along came All-Purpose Radar Broadcast power; television went three-dimensional and became teledar, inexpensive enough so that every Eskimo could own a set and, incidentally, the only industry where an actor might make a living.

As teledar took over entertainment household devices began to move around in the form of robots powered by APRB, rocket-ships piloted only by automatics made time-table flights to every planet in the system, and everyone agreed that man could hardly ask for more control over his environment.

So one fine day—oh, about the year 2208—

The doorscreen above the valuable antique radiator in Lester's living room fluoresced for a moment, then crackled into a picture of the husky man waiting outside the apartment. He wore the visored helmet of a service mechanic. An enormous yellow box beside him filled most of the doorscreen.

"Lester the Jester? Rholg's Robot Reorganizers. I have your butler-valet combo here all fitted with the special custom-built adjustments you ordered. You have to sign a danger-and-damage release before I can leave him."

"Uhm." The red-haired young man nodded and wiped the sleep from his eyes so that the worry could shine through. He rose from the couch, stretched jerkily. "I'd sign a life-and-liberty waiver to get what I need out of that robot. Hey, door," he called. "Twenty-three, there—twenty-three."

Swiftly the door slid up into its sandwiched recess. The mechanic flipped a switch on his beamlock and the huge crate floated delicately into the apartment, bumped gently to rest against a wall. Lester rubbed his hands nervously. "I hope—"

"You know, Mr. Lester, I never thought a guy like me would ever get to see you in person. In my line I meet all kinds of celebrities—like yesterday, when I returned two receptionist-robots to the police commissioner. We'd equipped them with lie-detectors and flat feet. But wait till

I tell my wife I met the biggest comedian in teledar! She always says, Mr. Lester—"

"Not Mr. Lester. Lester—Lester the Jester."

The mechanic grinned widely and appreciatively. "Like on the program, huh?" He pointed his beamlock at the crate, moving the switch from *carry* to *disrupt*. "And when one of the boys at the shop figured you were going to use this robot like a gagwriter I asked him would he like his head broken. I told him your jokes were strictly off the cuff—I heard. Right?"

"Right!" A very loud, vastly amused laugh. "Lester the Jester using a gagwriter! What kind of rumors—imagine that! Me, the glib sahib of ad-lib—as my fans like to call me—working from someone else's boffolas. *Such a thing!* Just because I thought it would be snappy for the hemisphere's top comedian to have a robot valet who can give with gags on demand. *Hah!* Well, let me see him."

A rattling whirr as directive force tore out of the beamlock, dissolving the yellow crate into quickly scattered dust. When it had settled they were looking at five feet of purple metal man.

"You changed his shape!" Lester yelped accusingly. "I sent you a smooth-lined twenty-two hundred and seven model with the new cylindrical trunk. You bring back a pear-shaped piece of machinery looking squeezed down—as if it had a paunch all the way around. And bowlegged!"

"Look, sir, the techs just had to expand his midsection. Even on microwire that file of jokes took up an awful lot of space. And your order said for him to be able to work out twists on the gags in the file—so they rassled up a new gimmick, what they call a variable modifier. More space, more weight. But let me turn him on."

The man in the visored helmet inserted a convoluted length of iridium—an Official Robot Master Key—into the back of the robot's neck. Two full clicking turns and machinery purred. Metal arms crossed upon a metal chest in the accepted gesture of servility. Eyebrow ridges clinked upward. Multilinked lips pursed questioningly.

"Migosh!" the mechanic marveled. "I never seen such a snooty expression on any face before."

"My fiancée, Josephine Lissy—she's the singer on my program—designed it," Lester told him proudly. "Her idea of what a butler-valet combo should look like—sort of in the ancient English tradition. She also thought up his name. Hey, Rupert, tell me a joke."

Rupert's mouth opened. His voice clacked out, rising and falling like a sine wave. "On what subject, sir?"

"Oh, anything. A vacation trip. A small belly-laugh joke."

"Ginsberg was making his first voyage to Mars," Rupert began. "He was shown to a small table in the salon and told that his tablemate would be a Frenchman. Since the other had not yet—"

The Rholg's mechanic leaned across his flat purple chest. "That's another gimmick—a meson filter. You said you wanted him able to distinguish between laugh-power in different gags so he could fit them to the audience. And price was no object. That's all you have to tell a tech. They knocked themselves out developing a gadget to do the job just right."

"If it does a couple of writers I know are going to be sorry pigeons. We'll see who's the comedian around here," Lester muttered. "Lester the Jester or Green and Anderson. Greedy little paper-spoilers!"

"—the Frenchman, noticing Ginsberg already at his meal, stopped. He clicked his heels and bowed from the waist. *'Bon appétit,'* he said. Ginsberg, not to be outdone, rose to *his*—"

"A meson filter is what they call it, eh? Well, even that bill in galactic figures your outfit sent me will be worth it if I can get what I want out of Rupert. But I wish you hadn't spoiled his looks!"

"—this succinct dialogue was repeated. Until, the day before the end of the voyage, Ginsberg sought the steward and asked him to explain the meaning of—"

"We'd have found some way of packaging all the stuff or at least distributing it better if you hadn't been in such a hurry. You wanted him back by Wednesday, no matter what."

"Yes, of course. I go on the waves tonight. I needed the—ah, stimulation Rupert would give me." Lester ran nervous fingers through his red hair. "He seems to be okay."

"—approached the Frenchman, who was already at table. He clicked his heels and bowed from the waist. *'Bon appétit,'* Ginsberg told him. Joyfully, the Frenchman leaped to his feet and—"

"Then you won't mind signing this. Regular release form. You take all responsibility for the actions of Rupert. I can't leave him here till I get it."

"Sure." Lester signed. "Anything else?"

"—'Ginsberg,' the Frenchman said!" Rupert had finished.

"Not bad. But I can't use it quite that way. We need a—Holy options, what's that?" Lester teetered backward.

The robot, standing perfectly immobile, was clacking wildly, grinding his gears and *pinging* wires as if he were coming apart.

"Oh, *that*." The man from Rholg's gestured. "That's another bug the techs didn't have time to clean up. Comes from the meson filter. Near as we can figure out it's what they call an after-effect of his capacity to distinguish between gags that are partly funny and gags that are very funny. Electronic differentiation of the grotesque, it says in the specifications—in a man, a sense of humor.

'Course, in a robot it only means there's a kink in the exhaust."

"Yeah. I hope he doesn't blow that at me when I have a hangover. A robot that laughs at his own jokes! *Whooee,* what a sound!" Lester shivered. "Rupert, go mix me one of those Three-Ply Lunar Landings."

The mass of purple metal turned and waddled off to the kitchen. Both men chuckled at his bow-legged teetering gait.

"Here's a couple of bucks for your trouble. Sorry I don't have more change on me. Like a carton of Star-Gazers? My sponsor keeps me stocked to the curls on them. Licorice, maple-walnut?"

"I sorta like my cigarettes flavored with crab-apple. The missus too—gee, thanks. Hope everything goes all right."

The service mechanic stuffed his beamlock into his tunic and left. Lester called, "Three-and-twenty," after him. The door slid down into place.

Rupert tottered back with an intricate spiral of transparent tubing filled with a yellow-and-white liquid. The comedian sucked the drink out rapidly, exhaled and combed his hair back into place.

"Right! That was delicious in its own foul way. Whoever built that master bartender unit into you really knew his electronics. Now look, I don't know just how to order you in this deal—though you're able to read now, come to think of it. Here's the script for tonight's teledar show, the straight part.

"Type a companion script for me based on each speech in the original that I've underlined, a gag variation on the statement. That's what I memorize to give the famous ad-lib effect—but you don't have to know that. Start typing."

Without a word, the robot flipped through the sheaf of papers handed to him, instantly "memorizing" on his microwire files every word in them.

Then he dropped the script on the floor again and walked over to the electric typewriter. He pushed the chair in front of it aside. His torso slid down his metallic legs until he was just at the right height for typing. He went to work. Paper boiled up out of the machine.

Lester watched admiringly. "If only his ideas are half as funny as they are fast—hello!" He picked the sheaf of typescript off the floor to which Rupert had returned and set it on a table. "Never did that before. Used to be the neatest piece of machinery on the planet, always picking up after me. But—well, genius has the right to be temperamental!" The phone buzzed almost affirmatively.

He grinned and caught the phone as it bounded into his hands. "Radio Central," said the mouthpiece. "Miss Josephine Lissy calling. Will you take it on your scrambler or on hers?"

"Mine. LY—one hundred thirty-four—YJ. Check."

"Yes sir. Here's your party."

The radio phone sputtered as it adjusted to Lester's personal scrambling system that meant privacy for a conversation on a wavelength shared by millions. A girl with hair as brightly carrotty as Lester's appeared in the tiny screen above the mouthpiece.

"Hi, Red," she smiled. "Know something? Jo loves Lester."

"Smart girl—smart. Wait a minute while I get you transferred. Looking at you on this thing strains my eyes— besides, there isn't enough of you."

He twirled a dial, translated the phone's vibrations into the frequency of the doorscreen. Then, while the instrument whizzed back into place on the ceiling, he made a similar adjustment on the doorscreen manual dials, setting it for interior reception.

Josephine Lissy's image was radiant above the imitation radiator as he sighed down into the couch.

"Look, funnyman, this is no love-call. I'll get right

down to the most recent mess. Green and Anderson have blabbed to Haskell."

"What!" He leaped to his feet. "I'll sue them! I can too—the mutual release they signed specified that my use of gag-writers was not to be made public."

She shrugged. "A lot that'll help you. Besides, they didn't publicize it—just told it to Haskell. You couldn't even prove *that*. All I got was grapevine to the effect that Haskell is screaming over to see you.

"Green and Anderson have convinced him that without memorizing their gag copy on the straight part of the show you won't even be able to ad-lib a burp. And Haskell is just scared that the first program under his sponsorship will be a flop."

Lester grinned. "Don't worry, Jo. With any luck—"

"My sacred aunt's favorite space-opera!" she squealed. "What's that?"

That was an ear-splitting series of clanks, bumps, singing metal and siren-like shrieks. Lester whirled.

Rupert had finished typing. He held the long sheet of completed copy between purple fingers and shook over it. *Whirr,* he went. *Glongety-glonk. Pingle, pingle, pingle. Ka-zam!* He sounded like a cement mixer inside a cement mixer.

"Oh, that's Rupert. He's got a kink in his exhaust—makes like a mindless sense of humor. Of course he isn't human but does he seem to go for his own stuff! Come here, Rupert!"

The robot stopped clattering and slid up his legs to his full height. He walked to the doorscreen.

"When did they bring him back?" Jo asked. "Did they put all the stuff in him that you—why, they've *ruined* him! He looks like a case of dropsy—as if he has an abdominal ruff! And that beautiful expression on his face I designed—it's all gone! He doesn't look superior anymore, just sad—very sad. Poor Rupert!"

"Your imagination," Lester told her. "Rupert can't change his expression even if he wanted to. It's all automatic, built in at the factory. Just because we call him by a name instead of the number cues we use on the rest of the household machinery doesn't mean he has feelings. Outside of his duties as a valet, which he performs as imaginatively as a watch tells time, he's just a glorified filing system with a wadjacallit—a variable modifier to select—"

"Oh, that isn't so. Rupert has feelings, don't you, Rupert?" she cooed at him in a small voice. "You remember me, Rupert? Jo. How are you, Rupert?" The robot stared silently at the screen.

"Of all the unquaint feminine conceits—"

There was a definite *clang* as Rupert's heels smote together. He bowed stiffly from the hips. "Gins—" he began to say. His head went down majestically, kept on going down. It hit the floor with a terrific *zok*.

Jo became almost hysterical. Lester flapped his arms against his sides. Rupert, the back of his paunch peak-high in the air, rested stolidly respectful, his body making a right-angled triangle with the floor.

"—berg," Rupert finished from where his face angled against the floor. He made no move to rise. He *whurgled* softly, reminiscently.

"Well?" Lester glowered at him. "Are you going to lie there and look silly all day? Get up!"

"H-he *c-can't*," Joe shrieked. "Th-they've shifted h-his center of gra-gravity and he can't get up. If you ever do anything as funny as that bow over the teledar you'll kill two hundred million innocent people!"

Lester the Jester grimaced and bent over his robot. He caught it round the shoulders and tugged. Very slowly, very reluctantly, Rupert straightened. He pointed at Jo's image on the screen.

"That ain't no lady," he enunciated metallically. "That's

gonna be your wife. *Or*—it may not be Hades but brother it's gonna be life! *Or*—she's not shady, she's only—"

"Can it!" Lester yelled. "And I do mean *can* it!"

He brooded while the robot went into another gear-clashing paroxysm. "My fine tile floor! The best mid-twentieth century floor in the whole tower and look at it! A dent the size of—"

Jo clucked at him. "I've told you a dozen times that they only used tiled floors in *bathrooms* in the forties and fifties. Mostly in bathrooms, anyway. And that imitation radiator and roll-top desk are from two widely separated periods—you just don't have a sense of the antique, Lester lad. Wait till we've signed a marriage contract with each other—I'll show you what a Roosevelt-era home really looks like. How are Rupert's gags—on paper, I mean?"

"Don't know yet. He's just finished the script." The screen fluoresced along an edge. "Better get off, Jo. Someone's at the door. Call for me before the 'cast at the usual time. Bye."

At a signal from his master, the robot scuttled to the door and *twenty-three'd* at it. Two things happened simultaneously—the service mechanic from Rholg's Custom-Built Robots walked in and Rupert's head *zokked* against the floor.

Lester sighed and pulled Rupert straight again. "I hope he isn't going to repeat that courtly gesture anytime someone comes here. I'll have shellholes all over the living room."

"Has he done that before? That's not good. Remember, all of his basic control units are in his head and a lot of them have just started meshing the new service patterns. He's liable to fracture a bearing and go choo-choo. Like me to take him back to the plant for recalibration?"

"No, I don't have time. I start 'casting in two hours.

That reminds me—did your techs build that word-scanner into his forehead?"

The mechanic nodded. "Sure. See that narrow green plate over his eyes? Just flip that to one side or have him do it whenever you want silent written transmission. The words will flow across like on a regular news sign. I came back for the key. Left it stuck in his neck and I'd be in one sweet fix if I got back to the factory without it."

"Take it. I thought you were somebody else." Lester turned to face the dumpy little man in a striped tunic who had just barged in through the open door. "Hello, Mr. Haskell. Would you have a seat? I'll be with you in a moment."

"Give me the key," the mechanic commanded. Rupert pulled the Official Robot Master Key out of the back of his neck and held it out. The mechanic reached for it. Rupert dropped it.

"Well, I'll be—" the man from Rholg's started. "If I didn't know better, I'd swear he did it on purpose." He bent down to retrieve the key.

As his fingers closed over it, Rupert's right hand flicked forward slightly. The man jumped to his feet and sprang backwards through the doorway.

"No you don't!" he snarled. "Did you see what he was trying to do? Why—"

"Three-and-twenty," said Rupert. The door slid shut, cutting off the service mechanic's last statement. The robot came back into the apartment, clacking ever so slightly. His facial expression seemed even sadder than before— somehow disappointed.

"Two of those Lunar Landing specials," his master told him. He waddled off to prepare them.

"Now look here, Lester," John Haskell boomed in a voice surprising for his size. "I'll come right to the point. I didn't know you were using writers until Green and Anderson told me you'd fired them because they wouldn't take a cut in salary. I go with them when they say they've made you the highest paid comedian in United Americas. Now this show tonight is only an option of a—"

"Wait up, sir. I wrote my own stuff before they came to work for me and they operated entirely from my personal gag files. I fired them because they demanded a higher percentage of my earnings than I got. I can still ad-lib faster than any standup man in the business."

"I don't care whether you ad-lib or whether the stuff comes to you in a dream! I just want laughs on my program to get people in a proper frame of mind to hear my commercials. No, that's not what I mean—oh!" He reached out and grabbed one of the convoluted masses that Rupert had brought in and drained it rapidly. His face didn't even change color. "Not strong enough. Tasteless. Needs stuff."

The robot held the returned and empty receptacle for a moment and studied it. Then he bow-legged it back to the kitchen.

Lester decided that he didn't agree with the president of Star-Gazers, Inc. This drink had *wowie* in every alcoholic drop. But the drinks at the Planetmasters Club where Haskell lived were reputedly powerful.

"All I care about is this," Haskell was saying. "Can you work up a funny program tonight without Green and Anderson or can't you? You may have a high comic rating but they're spreading the word: people hear what they say in the industry. If Star-Gazers fail to pick up your thirteen-week option tonight after the trial 'cast for our product, you'll have to go back to daytime soap operas."

"Sure, Mr. Haskell, sure. But take a look at this script and *then* make your comments." Lester plucked the long sheet of copy out of the electric typewriter and handed it to the little man.

Dangerous, that. It might stink seven ways from Monday. But he hadn't had time to read it himself. Rupert had better be good!

He was, to judge from Haskell's reaction. The president of Star-Gazers had roared himself into the antique swivel-chair and sat there shaking. "Wonderful!" he wiped the tears from his eyes. *"Terrific!* Almost but not quite, colossal! I apologize, Lester. You don't need any gag-writers, you really do write comedy. Think you can memorize this before the program?"

"Shouldn't be any trouble. I always have to use a little infra-scopolamine for a rush job anyway. And in case I need an ad-lib suddenly I've got my robot."

"Robot? You mean him?" Mr. Haskell gestured to where Rupert stood *whirring* over his shoulder as he stared at the script. He pulled a dark spiral of tubing out of the purple hand, sucked at it.

"Yes, he has a gag file in his mid-section. He'll stand out of camera range and anytime I need a gag I just look at him and the words are spelled out on the forehead scanner. Had it all inserted in my butler-valet combo by the Rholg—Mr. Haskell! What's the matter?"

Haskell had dropped the tube. It lay on the floor, a thin wisp of black smoke steaming out of the open end. "Th-the drink," Haskell said hoarsely. His face, after experimenting with red, green and lavender for a while, compromised and settled on all three in a sort of alternated mottled arrangement. "Where's your—your—"

"In there! Second door to the left!"

The little man scurried off, his body low. He seemed to have lost all of his bones.

"Now what can—" Lester sniffed at the spiral drinking tube. My God! He was abruptly aware that Rupert was going *whirretty-whirretty-klonk.* "Rupert, what did you put in that drink?"

"He asked for something stronger, more tasty—"

"What did you put in that drink?"

The robot considered. "Five parts—(*whizz-clang*)—castor oil to three parts—(*bing-bong*)—Worcestershire sauce to—(*tinkle-tinkle-burr-r-r*)—four parts essence of red pepper—(*g-r-rang*)—to one part Cro—"

Lester whistled and the phone leaped into his hand. "Radio Central? Hospital emergency and I mean emerge! Lester the Jester, Artist's Tower, apartment one thousand and six. Hurry!" He ran down the hall to help his guest sit on his stomach.

When the interne saw the brightly-colored mess Haskell was becoming, he shook his head. "Let's get him in the stretcher and out!"

Rupert stood in the corner of the living room as the stretcher, secure in the grip of the interne's beamlock, floated through the door. "Musta been something he et," he clacked.

The interne glared back. "A comedian!"

Lester hurriedly drank three Lunar Landings. He mixed them himself. He had just finished memorizing the robot's ad-lib script with the aid of a heavy dose of infra-scopolamine when Jo breezed in. Rupert opened the door for her. *Clang. Zok.*

"You know, he's been doing this all day," Lester told her as he tugged the robot upright again. "And not only is he adding an original design to my floor but I suspect that he's not helping his bedamned mental processes any. Of course, he's obeyed *me* completely so far and all of his practical jokes have been aimed at others. . . ."

Rupert rolled something around in his mouth. Then he pursed his lips. Multilinked wrinkles appeared in his cheeks. He spat.

A brass hexagonal nut bounced against the floor. The three of them stared at it. Finally, Jo raised her head.

"What practical jokes?"

Lester told her.

"*Whew!* You're lucky your contract has a personal

immunity clause. Otherwise Haskell could sue you from Patagonia to Nome. But he still won't feel any affection for you, any *real* affection. He'll probably live, though. Get into your costume."

As Lester hustled into his spangled red suit in the next room, he called at her, "What're you singing tonight?"

"Why don't you come to a rehearsal sometime and find out?"

"Have to keep up my impromptu reputation. What is it?"

"Oh, 'Subjective Me, Objective You' from Googy Garcia's latest hit—*Love Among the Asteroids*. This robot of yours may write good comedy but he sure is a bust as a butler. The junk he leaves scattered around. Paper, cigarettes, drink-tubes! When I enter your life on a permanent basis, young feller..." Her voice died as she bent and began picking up the litter from the floor of the living room. Behind her Rupert meditated at her back. *"Whirr?"* he went.

His right hand flashed up. He came at her fast. He reached her.

"Yeeee-eeee!" Jo screamed as she climbed halfway up the opposite wall. She turned as she came down. Her eyes literally crackled.

"Who—what—" she began menacingly. Then she noticed Rupert standing, his hand still out, all of his machinery going *whistle-clong-ka-bankle* all at once.

"Why, he's laughing at me! Think it funny do you, you mechanical pervert?" She sped at him in fury, her right hand going far back for a terrific slap.

Lester had torn out of the kitchen when she screamed. Now he saw her hand whistling around in a great arc almost at Rupert's face.

"Jo!" he yelled. "Not in the head!"

Moing-g-g-g-g-g!

"Think you'll be all right, Miss Lissy," the doctor said. "Just keep your hand in this cast for two weeks. Then we'll X-ray again."

"Let's get started for the studio, Jo," Lester said nervously. "We'll be late. Shame this had to happen."

"Isn't it though? But before I let you accompany me anywhere I want to get one thing straight. You get rid of Rupert."

"But, Jo darling, honey, sweet, do you know what a writer he is?"

"I don't care. I wouldn't think of bringing children up in a home that he infested. According to the Robot Laws you have to keep him at home. I frankly think he's gone dotty in a humorous way. But I don't like it. So—you'll have to choose between me and that gear-happy gagman." She smoothed the cast on her arm as she waited for his reply.

Now Rupert, in his present condition—for all of his eccentricities—meant that Lester's career as a comedian was assured, that never again would he have to worry about material, that he was set for life. On the other hand, he doubted he'd ever meet a woman who was as close to what he wanted in a wife as Jo. She was—well, Lester's ideal—she alone among the girls he knew met his requirements for a successful marriage.

It was a clear choice between money and the woman he loved.

"Well," Lester told Jo at last. "We can still be good friends?"

Jo was finishing her song by the time he arrived at the studio. She didn't even glower at him as she walked away from the camera-mikes. The commercial began.

Lester stationed Rupert against the wall of the control booth where no camera could pick up a view of his purple body. Then he joined the other actors under the dead camera who were waiting for the end of the commercial before starting their combination drama and comedy.

The announcer came to the end of the last rolling syllable of admiration. The five Gloppus sisters came up for the finale:

> S—G—F, F, C!
> Star-Gazer's Fifteen Flavored Cigarettes!
> Stay away from tastes like hay!
> Days are gay with nasal play,
> Star-Gazer's Fifteen Flavored Way!
> S—G—F, F, C! From choc-o-late—to chereeee!

The camera above Lester sparked colors as he and the actors took over. A simple playlet—romance in a fueling station on Phobos. Lester was extraneous to the plot—he merely came in with gags from time to time, gags based on some action or line in the straight story.

Good gags tonight—even the program manager was laughing. Well, not laughing—but he *smiled* now and then. And, buddy, if a program manager smiles, then people all over the western hemisphere have collapsed into a cataleptic hysteria. This is a fact as demonstrably certain and changeless as that the third vice-president of a teledar corporation shall always be the butt of the very worst jokes or, as it is known sociologically, the Throttlebottom Effect.

From time to time Lester glanced at his robot. The creature was not staring at him always—that was annoying. He had turned to examine the interior of the control booth through the transparent door which shut it off from the rest of the studio. Lester had removed the narrow green plate from above Rupert's eyes in case an ad-lib were necessary.

One was suddenly necessary. The second ingenue worked her way into a line beginning, "So when Harold said he had come to Mars to get away from militarism and regimentation"—and expired into a frantic "I told him—I told him—um, I had to tell him that—that—" She gaped, snapped her fingers spasmodically as she tried to remember.

Out of camera range, the prompter's fingers flew over the keys of the silent typewriter which projected the entire line on a screen above their heads. Meanwhile there was dead air. Everyone waited for Lester to make a crack that would fill the horrible space.

He spun to his robot. Thankfully he noticed that Rupert was staring at him. Good! Now if he could only meson-filter an ad-lib!

Words flowed across the screen on Rupert's forehead. Lester read them off as fast as they appeared.

"Say, Barbara, why don't you tell the station manager to switch from atomics to petroleum?"

"I don't know," she said, feeding the line back like a good straight-man while she memorized the passage she had forgotten. "Why should I tell him to switch from atomics to petroleum?"

From the corner, Rupert roared, "Because there's no fuel like an oil fuel!"

The studio guffawed. Rupert guffawed. Only he sounded as if he were coming apart. All over United Americas, people grabbed at their teledar sets and tried to hold them together as the electronic apparatus *klunked, pingled* and *whirrety-whirred.*

Even Lester laughed. Beautiful! A lot more sophisticated than the crud he'd been getting from Green and Anderson, yet mixed with the pure old Iowa corn on which all belly-laughter is based. The robot was—

Hey! Rupert hadn't fed him that line—he'd used it himself. People weren't laughing at Lester the Jester—they were laughing at Rupert, even if they couldn't see him. *Hey-y-y!*

When the playlet ended the camera-mikes shifted to Josephine Lissy and the orchestra.

Lester took advantage of the break to charge up to Rupert. He pointed imperiously at the control booth.

"Get inside, you topper-copper, and don't come out until I'm ready to leave. Save the punch-line for yourself, will you? Bite the hand that oils you? Git, damn you, git!"

Rupert moved back a pace, almost crushing a property man. *"Bing-bing?"* he chuckled inquiringly. *"Honk-beeper-bloogle?"*

"No, I'm not kidding," Lester told him. "Get inside that control booth and stay there!"

With a dragging step that cut a thin groove in the plastic floor, Rupert went off to St. Helena.

Going on with the show, Lester watched him take his place behind the technicians, his shoulders slumped in a dejection the smoothlined 2207 model was never designed to register. From time to time he noticed the robot stride jerkily about the tiny booth, the word-scanner in his forehead making such abortive efforts as "Why is hyperspace like a paperweight?" and "When is a mutant not a mutant?" Lester indignantly ignored these attempts to make amends.

The mid-program commercial—"Have you ever asked yourself," the announcer put it to them, "why among the star-blazers it's Star-Gazers one thousand to one? Impartial tests show that these adventurous seekers in empty space always prefer—*what in*—"

Rupert slammed the door shut behind the last of three angry control technicians. Then he began pulling switches. He turned dials.

"He just up and threw us out!"

"That robot's gone psycho! Listen, he can shift the control to the inside of the booth. It's very simple. Is he a talking robot—no, please God!"

"Yeah! He can broadcast himself! Can he talk?"

"Can he!" Lester groaned. "Better blast him out fast!"

"Blast him?" An engineer laughed painfully. "He's locked the door. And do you know what the doors and walls of that booth are made of? He can stay in there until we get clearance from the IPCC. Which—"

"You know why they call them Star-Gazers, don't you?" Rupert's voice boomed over the teledar speaker which carried through the studio and incidentally all through the western hemisphere. "One puff and you're flat on your back! *Wongle-wangle-ding-ding!* Yes sir, you see stars all right—all colors. You smoke 'em and novas go off in your head. *Gr-r-rung! Ka-bam-ka-blooie!* Fifteen flavors and all of them worth a raspberry! *Zingambong—*"

The walls of the control booth shivered with huge scraping laughter. And not only the walls were shivering.

Jo soothed Lester as best she could.

"He can't go on forever, darling. He's got to stop!"

"Not with that file he has—and that variable modifier—and that meson-filter. I'm through. I'll never 'cast again—they'll never let me in anywhere. And I don't know how to do anything else. No other skills, no other experience. I'm through for life, Jo!"

The engineers finally had to shut off all power in Teledar City. That meant all 'casting stopped, including messages to space-ships and emergency calls to craft on the ground. It meant that elevators in the building stopped between floors, that lights went out in government offices all over the tower. Then they were able to open the doors with an auxiliary remote control unit and drag the inert robot out.

When the radiant power was shut off, so was he.

So Lester married Jo. But he didn't live happily ever after. He was barred from teledar for life.

He didn't starve, though. He wished he had from time

to time. Because the 'cast that ruined him made Rupert. People wrote in demanding to hear more of this terrific robot who kidded the crass off sponsors. And Star-Gazers tripled their sales. Which, after all, is the ultimate test . . .

Lester manages Rupert the Rollicking Robot—("The screwiest piece of machinery since the invention of the nut"). He lives with him too, has to by Robot Law. He can't sell him—who'd want to get rid of their only source of bread and marmalade? And he can't hire anyone to take care of Rupert—anyone in his right mind, that is. But worst of all Lester has to *live* with Rupert. He finds it difficult.

Once a week he visits Jo and his children. He looks very haggard then. Rupert's practical jokes get more complicated all the time.

■ **CONFUSION CARGO** ■

CAPTAIN ANDREAS STEGGO had commanded a light neg-ship in the late war before peace and retirement had given him the master's position aboard the Sagittarian Line's *Reward*. He was big, slightly brutal and accustomed to absolute obedience from his crews.

On the other hand, the crew hastily signed on by the Aldebaranian office were all ex-cargo jockeys of the twenty-five-planet system thrown out of work by the sudden cessation of hostilities. They were rough, fast-thinking and terrifically independent.

Excepting myself, there were no passengers. The voyage was to be especially long—two months; the cargo was particularly nasty—ten tons of stinking viscodium.

Anyone with half an ounce of brain would have known there would be trouble. Unfortunately the requirements for an official of the Sagittarian Line include a university degree and galactic license; nothing about half an ounce of brain.

First we discovered the viscodium, instead of being sealed in dellite drums, was stored in a large tank with an overflow lid. That made for economy in shipping space, but also for certain discomfort in such useful functions as breathing. I'd lie awake at sleep period thinking of what would happen if the lid fell off and the green slime came churning through the loose hatches.

Then one of the loading pipes developed a leak under the strain of acceleration. The *Reward* was an old ship and she had been hastily serviced for this, her first trip in five years. Breen, the ship's welder, burst the pipe while repairing it and we tossed him, stiff within the congealed mass of viscodium, through an air-lock. No second welder either; so when the plumbing . . .

After the burial service, a delegation from the crew visited Captain Steggo and accused him of negligence in not having the loading pipes inspected for residual viscodium immediately after the take-off. They demanded their protest be logged. Steggo had all five of them clapped in restrainons. He then announced that full-dress discipline would be observed until we arrived; all ship's officers were to go armed at all times. I heard angry men in cheap *hwat* suits muttering after that about punishment half-meals and longer watches for a smaller active crew.

Mr. Skandelli, the chief engineer, visited me and offered a sawed-off shmobber. I looked at the foot-long weapon and declined. "Never touch the stuff."

"More than this may be touched before we warp in," he said grimly. "When Aldebaranian riff-raff gets snappish, I start using the armory. And passengers are classed with officers."

"That's no compliment on the *Reward*."

He looked at me, holstered the shmobber and left.

An hour later, I was presented with the captain's compliments and asked to attend him on the bridge. The whole business was beginning to annoy me more than slightly, but under the peculiar circumstances of my status I didn't feel like arousing any unnecessary antagonism. I went, determined not to be enlisted on either side—if it had come to choosing sides.

Steggo overflowed a huge armchair. A faint stubble

covered his chin which, considering the cheapness of a depilosac, was unnecessarily filthy.

"Mr. Skandelli tells me you have no desire to be classed with the officers. However," he waved a huge paw to forestall my objections, "that's beside the point. You are Dr. R. Sims, late of Naval Research?"

"Yes. Robert Sims, physical chemist grade 2, Aldebaranian Project CBX-19329." I tried to keep my voice from quavering. This man wanted to bollix my papers.

He smiled and studied my questionnaire. "I am interested, Dr. Sims, in why a person of your standing chooses to travel on an uncomfortable cargo ship when the fastest negships and government cruisers are at his disposal."

"I am going home to visit my family whom I haven't seen in more than three years." I hoped my voice sounded confident. "Naval employees are not allowed aboard negships for matters of personal convenience. It would be six months before obtainable priorities would get me a cabin on a reconverted liner. Since my leave starts immediately, the *Reward* looked damn good."

Papers rustled as he held them up to the light. "The seal is genuine enough. Ordinarily, the matter would not have come to my attention. But remember, we are still traveling under the mercantile sections of the articles of war. After your amazing outburst to Mr. Skandelli—who approached you at my instigation, by the way—I thought you merited looking into."

"I told Mr. Skandelli what any passenger in his right mind would have. Having paid for my passage, my protection is in your hands and not in mine." I touched the door button. "May I go?"

"One moment." He turned his massive head slowly. "Mr. Ballew, bring in the prisoners."

Ballew was the astrogator. He was a thin fair-haired fellow who had been hunched over his charts during the interview. He grimaced and left, returning in a few seconds with five men.

The first of them was the tallest man I'd ever seen, not excluding the captain. The yoke of the restrainon about his neck barely seemed able to cover his body with its lines of force. His head was free to permit breathing, and the machine had been adjusted above his knees, enabling him to shuffle along in an odd, broken-legged fashion. The other four were likewise yoked.

Steggo introduced them to me.

"Ragin, whom I have logged as the leader of an abortive mutiny. The other woebegone gentlemen have names I either can't pronounce or don't choose to remember."

I waited, wondering how I came into this situation.

Suddenly the tall man spoke. The words seemed to come with difficulty because of the restrainon pressing upon his diaphragm. "You'll remember us, Steggo, if I have to hunt you straight across the galaxy."

The captain smiled. "A shmobber squad on earth will quiet you. And it *will* be shmobbers for you after my report is in."

Ragin glared and shuffled rapidly across the small room. His intention was obviously to hurl himself against the captain. Steggo lurched out of his chair and placed it in front of the moving man. Ragin hit the chair, bounced off it and was hurled against a bulkhead. I heard the thud as his head smashed into metal. The astrogator helped him to his feet.

"That, too, will go into the log," Steggo puffed. "Now, Dr. Sims, if you will please come this way."

I followed him, disagreeably conscious of the murderous thoughts swirling about in the bridge.

He walked to the ship's visor, fiddled with the dial and snapped it on. I gasped.

"That, as you see, is the hold. I was looking through at the hold where our Mr. Ragin and his little playmates were being kept. I thought I saw somebody bending over Ragin, feeding him. Mr. Skandelli was sent to investigate with the second officer and my suspicions were proven correct. The ship was then searched and six others found. Five of these are the wives of these men here; two belong to other members of the crew who are now being placed in restrainons themselves."

"Women!" I muttered. "Aboard a ship. Stowaways!"

"Ah, you are familiar with the mercantile sections of the articles of war. 'Any person of the feminine gender found aboard a ship engaged in interstellar flight without naval or military guard shall be subject to death or such other punishment as a court martial may direct.' That is the law, is it not?"

"But captain," I protested. "That law was directed against members of the Fino Feminist League who cooperated with the enemy during the war. It has never been used against civilians."

"Which is not to say it does not apply to civilians. I am fully aware that women have participated in our government during the entire conflict and even served with distinction during the Battle of the Dead Star. But the law is specific. It considers the costly sabotage at the time we were attacked and forbids women aboard ships on a blanket basis."

His heavy face seemed unusually thoughtful. He snapped off the visor.

"What do you want me to do?"

He pointed to the open log. "I've entered the entire incident; the fact that these men and two others, prior to the attempt at mutiny, did willfully smuggle their wives on board, in knowing violation by all parties concerned of space law." Ragin snorted heavily in the background. "I want you to sign the entry, testifying to the physical presence on ship of these women."

"But I'm not an officer. I'm not even an employee of the line!"

"That is precisely why I want your signature. It provides disinterested evidence. If you refuse, in the light of the emergency conditions now revealed as well as your semi-official naval status, I shall be forced to conclude you favor the mutinous elements. You will then be placed—"

He didn't have to finish. I signed.

Steggo followed me courteously to the door. "Thank you, Dr. Sims. Mr. Ballew, please assemble the court-martial."

Ballew had turned a fiery red. "But, sir, you aren't going to court-martial them before we reach Earth!"

"I am, Mr. Ballew. And you will sit on the court. Remember the mercantile sections: 'Any merchant ship in priority categories 1AA, 1AB or 1AC, whether proceeding with or without military or naval escort, shall be considered to be on military or naval status for the purpose of discipline at the discretion of the master.' A viscodium cargo is sufficiently delicate to place us in category 1AC. And our dendro drive prohibits radio communication even if a ship this size carried an interstellar transmitter, which it doesn't. Please assemble the court."

As Ballew, breathing hard, hurried from the bridge, I thought of what a space lawyer we had for a captain. He'd probably been an administration officer until near the end when the bottom of the barrel was carefully scraped. Early retirement usually pointed to such a background. Mr. Discipline, himself!

"You appreciate the fact, captain, that the priority categories as well as the mercantile sections which you quote so glibly were all wartime measures?"

"I do. Wartime measures which have not yet been repealed. Now, Dr. Sims, if you would return to your cabin?"

I left, trying to throw some passing comfort at Ragin

while the door closed behind me. He was staring at my parplex jumper oddly, his brows knitted as if he were trying to decide something very important. I was wearing the naval *pi* with three palms.

My cabin had been searched. Officers or crew? I didn't know. It was no fun being a neutral, as many small and sorrowful planets have discovered.

The suitcase and toilet articles had been hastily rifled, clumsily put back into place. I felt the head of the bed. The invisible blusterbun still reposed on the top of the ledge. Obviously no search scanners or even colored powder had been employed.

Amateurs. A stellective would have used powder, at least.

I pocketed the tiny, completely transparent weapon and stretched out on the bed. My toilet articles caught my eye. The half-empty container of depilosac had been probed for hidden articles. White drippings of the stuff stained the red shelf. Well, they hadn't found anything there.

Nothing incriminating had been found in the suitcase either; I had selected its contents with great care. Rather a nice touch that, choosing something old-fashioned like a suitcase instead of a modern space-saving collapsicon.

But if this mess got down to really sharp brass tacks, all my precautions wouldn't be worth a gram of plutonium in an atomic furnace. Damn Steggo anyway. Damn him and his mercantile sections. Damn Ragin. Damn the war.

I fell asleep in a wave of homesickness for Earth.

Weapons coughed brokenly at the stern of the ship. I came awake with my hand on the blusterbun. Somebody ran past my cabin screaming. The lights went off, came back on, then went off again.

I hit the floor of the bed as my pneumastic mattress was turned off too. Something rattled against the outside bulkhead and passed down the spaceship. Meteor dust? Not this far out. Probably Steggo turning on the gas sprinkler system. Or the mutineers.

So this was a mutiny. I had been in an atomic explosion and a devastating space negation in my time. I had been in the photonite plant on Rigel VIII when molecular joint lubricant was spilled against the dome, allowing our air to leak out into space. Now I was in a mutiny.

Fingers tapped on my door in a frantic message. I threw it open.

The man lying outside was evidently a crew member. He had a gaping, smoking hole instead of his chest.

"Jobal!" he almost whispered. "Please, please Jobal—" He seemed to belch; when he didn't move I realized it was a death rattle. I moved his hand gently and closed the door. I went back to the side-board of the bed and sat down.

Who was Jobal? A friend? His wife, sweetheart? One of his gods? I must have sat in the darkness for an hour. After a while I noticed the ship was silent again. There was only the rolling hum of the Dendros.

Footsteps became louder and stopped outside my door. There was the sound of a man stepping over the body. Then the door was flung open and two huge Aldebaranians strode in. They leveled still-throbbing shmobbers at my waist.

"Captain Ragin wants to see you."

There. So the score was in. And now I imagined, all bets were being paid. And which side was I supposed to be on? I walked carelessly to the door, keeping the pocket in which I had the blusterbun away from them.

Ragin sat in Steggo's chair. He didn't fill it as completely, but he looked just as dominant as the captain. Ballew pored over his charts in a corner. Except for the splash of blood on the floor, the room was as I had left it.

"Hello, Dr. Sims," Ragin grinned through puffed lips. Ballew didn't look up. "Some changes been made."

"For the better, I hope." I waited.

"Yeah. We think so." He looked behind me at my guards. "He's been searched?"

"Well—" one of them began.

"We didn't think—" the other fumbled.

"Great exploding novas! What do you blastheads think this is—a meeting of the Aldebaranian Benevolent Association?" He was on his feet snarling at them, his head almost two feet above mine.

"I can save you the trouble—er, Captain." I flipped the blusterbun from my pocket and held it out, butt foremost.

He stared uncomprehendingly at my outstretched hand for a few moments. Then he reached forward gingerly and took the invisible weapon.

A smile twisted his mouth as he ran his fingers over its intricacies. "Well, I'll be washed by a comet's tail! A blusterbun! Dainty and deadly. I've heard about these things but I never hoped to have one. How does a civilian rate it?"

"Naval research," I reminded him.

Coolly, he appraised me. "Maybe. Maybe not. I'll still have to have you searched." The guards came up.

I moved away. "Now, wait a moment. I gave you my weapon. Had I wanted to, I could have shot you with the same motion before your zombie friends decided to swallow or wipe their mouths. I carry documents on my person that I most definitely don't want seen until I reach Earth. Unless I'm mistaken, you want some favor of me. If you read those documents, all deals are automatically off; and you'll be in a mess about five times as disagreeable as a mutiny."

He took time to chew on that. Finally: "O. K. Not that you can kill more than one man even if you have another weapon. If you start shooting, you'll be thoroughly butchered. And we do want a good deed out of you."

A tall, blonde woman came in with a tray. She prodded

me with it. Catching on, I took a cup of hot liquid. Aldebaranian *hialiau juice*. Things were looking up.

"Elsa and I were just married. I wasn't going to leave her to what that fat sadist calls justice. The boys were all for mutiny thirty-six hours after we cleared Booma City, but I held them down until our wives were discovered. We've been miners and independent freightmen; we're not used to this sort of disciplinary guff."

My chin pointed at the red mess on the floor. "Steggo?"

"No. One of our boys. We've been careful to keep this a completely bloodless mutiny as far as the officers were concerned. As a result, there've been more casualties on our side than there should have been. We lost four men."

"Five," one of my guards broke in. "There was another stiff outside this guy's cabin. Couldn't see in the dark, but it felt like Rildek."

Ragin nodded. "Five, then. We'll have a roll call after we get the power turned back on. Running the ship on auxiliaries now. Now what I want you to do, doctor, is sign a document testifying to the background of the mutiny as you know it, as well as an affidavit stating that when last seen by you Steggo and his officers were all alive and in as good condition as could be expected."

"If I see them in that state, I will."

"You will. We're letting them go in a small lifeboat, with enough to last until they reach a base. If you want to, you may join them. This *is* a mutinous ship."

"No, thank you." I tried to sound casual. "I'll stay here."

He studied me. "I thought you'd say that. There's something terrifically phony about you, doctor, but I don't have time to figure it out."

I smiled. "I'm grateful for your lack of time." Then I put my cup on the floor. "But your word on this. I can take your word, because the fact you didn't kill Steggo and his officers indicates that you don't intend to turn pirate. Whatever your plans may be, will you tell me on your honor that you will see to it that I eventually reach Earth or Earth's authority?"

He pumped my hand in a pulverizing grip. "Word of honor. On my honor as a—a mutineer." We both grinned.

On the way to the air lock, the man behind me suddenly pushed his shmobber into my back. Startled, I stopped.

"My idea," Ragin said. "When Steggo reaches civilization, he'll tell the story his way. I want him to think you were detained aboard by force. It'll give your testimony more legality and protect you as well. I don't think you want to be investigated."

I thanked him. Quite a guy, this Ragin.

Ex-Captain Steggo, Chief Engineer Skandelli, and five other officers lay on the floor of the little lifeboat, restrainon yokes about their necks. The fat man glared up madly.

"Cast me adrift in a small boat will you, Ragin? Well, I'll pull through somehow. I'll see you dissolving under the biggest thermons in the galactic navy!"

My guard bent over and spat in his face.

"You'll pull through, all right," Ragin said soberly. "You have twelve collapsicons containing every conceivable need." He smiled. "And after you we get rid of that unholy viscodium."

He made rapid adjustments on the restrainons, setting them to automatically turn off the binding lines of force within a half-hour. As he stooped over Skandelli, I noticed the chief was wearing a bandage over his chest.

"Do you want to make a little bet, fellow?" the engineer said softly. "I'll bet you my arms against your guts that before we're picked up you'll be warming a cot in a Terran prison."

Ragin smiled down at him. "Now that's no way to talk, Skandelli. After you locked yourself in the Dendros and gave my men all that trouble in blasting you out! Some of them had such nice plans for you; they'd just adore keeping you on the *Reward* to play with."

Skandelli turned a creamy white and shut up.

"All set. Get ready to cast off. This guy," he indicated me, "stays with us. So does Ballew. They're hostages."

As the air lock closed, I heard Steggo's wild shriek, "Dr. Sims, we'll be back, we'll be back, we'll be—"

There was a *whoosh* as the life boat arced away.

Ballew typed the papers on the basis of Ragin's written notes. We were alone on the bridge. Obviously, we were trusted.

I looked at Ballew's sullen, pale face. He was young for an officer, even aboard a cargo ship. What was in this for him? I asked him.

"Oh, I don't know," he said, rolling the last sheet out of the machine. "I ran away to sea first because I'd read a lot of books. The great ancients: Conrad, London, Nordhoff and Hall. Then I read books about space—*Mallard's Travels,* Soose, Jon Iim. So I thought I was in too limited a medium and went to astrogation school. But space is as dull as the sea."

I clucked sympathetically and ran my fingers over the smooth finish of the chair. "Things generally are, to a romantic. And you expected to find something really interesting in a mutiny?"

He flushed and I remembered how he had looked when the captain had been roaring at him. "Nothing like that. I knew Ragin on Aldebaran VI—Nascor, that is—and I'd gone on a couple of hunting trips to Aldebaran XVIII with some of the other members of the crew. When I signed on as astrogator I told them of the crew shortage and they came a-running. I even helped them stow their wives aboard." He stared at me defiantly.

Of course, I nodded to show I thought this was no crime under the circumstances. The boy went on.

"I'd never traveled with Steggo before, but I'd heard of

him. When he started to pull this mercantile section stuff, I told Rildek and Gonda—Gonda was the guy watching over you all the time—and they passed the word. Tore in here in the middle of the court-martial and took over the ship. Steggo was planning to toss those guys and their women through an air lock!"

"Not a particularly nice thing to do, but the Fino Feminists did manage to wreck three squadrons at the beginning of the war. These men knew that women are strictly forbidden to be present on a ship without official escorts; why in the name of the Curvature did they bring them?"

He shrugged. "Well, they wanted to build a home in a system where every foot of ground wasn't worth its weight in galactic credits. Aldebaran is almost all ore and almost all staked out. The Solarian asteroids have become pretty cheap during the war; they thought they'd pool their capital and buy one. But the women had to come or they'd be spending half their capital on fares. Aldebaran-Sol is an expensive trip."

"Don't I know!" I read the stuff he had typed and signed it. "Now I imagine they plan to hole out on Otho or one of the obscure little suns near it."

The papers were tucked in the astrogator's desk. "Don't know where exactly, except that it must be an uninhabited system and preferably unexplored. You'll be set on a course for Sol. If the ship is found in good condition and no murders are committed, the affair doesn't come under the jurisdiction of the galactic navy, especially since it's being demobilized. And you know how much time the Aldebaranian Patrol will spend on a mutiny."

"About as much time as it takes to move the papers from the 'missing in space' to the 'wanted for mutiny' file. But you'll have trouble over women. Only seven of them."

"Maybe." He stretched and the blue parplex tightened over a meager chest. "The galaxy is big and business will be sun-bent for expansion after the war. We'll always be able to slip off and get a job somewhere when things cool off."

Ragin came in heavily and thumbed through the charts. He selected one of them and studied it, swearing softly to himself.

Ballew looked at him inquiringly and continued. "Me, I have the satisfaction of helping my friends against a son of a bilge pump. I also get to know whether life on a desert planetoid is all it's cracked up to be."

"You'll get to know what a thermon tastes like," the tall man snarled suddenly. "Sol was this ship's original course, eh?"

The fair-haired kid had jumped to his feet. "Y-yes," he stuttered. "B-but I th-thought you could operate steering Dendros. I laid out a new course and all you had to do was steer to it."

"We can operate steering Dendros, all right," Ragin sneered. "When they're steerable." His hand flashed up, holding emptiness. My blusterbun.

"After you, doctor. I hope for your sake you *are* a physical chemist."

I walked ahead of him to the engine room. He gestured me inside. I was not feeling exactly immortal just then.

There was a little bubble of men around the double mass of convoluted machinery in the center. The bubble disintegrated as we came up and I stared at the green transparency for two minutes before I understood.

"Skandelli!" I shouted. "That's what he meant by that threat in the life boat. And that's what I heard rushing by the outside bulkhead during the mutiny."

"Yeah. The rotten bushaleon holed up in here for an hour. One of the loading pipes runs under the floor plates to the storage tank. He blasted a piece out of it and as soon as the holding pressure went down far enough, the stuff came crawling out over the Dendros. Of course, it congealed faster than it could come out of the small opening so at least the ship wasn't flooded. Not that it makes much difference to us."

I squatted and touched the cold stuff experimentally. Hard as dendraloid itself. "I'm afraid you're out of luck, Ragin. You can't steer with clogged Dendros, and if I know viscodium, you'll never get them unclogged. This ship goes to Sol."

"Maybe the ship does," he said easily. "But you don't."

Their set faces frightened me. "I have your word of honor! And I thought you were one man who wouldn't break it."

"I'm sorry, doctor, but this is one time when my word will have to be plumb disintegrated. We gave most of our high-neutron fuel to that bunch in the life-boat and we couldn't hope to make an uninhabited system unless we brought the ship close to it first. If we get to Sol I might be able to cook up something like an atomic explosion to account for Steggo and his officers as well as the five crew members who were shmobbered off.

"Ballew will back me up. As an officer, his testimony will be useful. *If* we all tell our stories straight, and *if* Steggo hasn't been picked up yet, we *might* be able to get away with it. But you're an outsider; we could never take a chance on your suddenly remembering what your civics teacher said. No, you either unstick those Dendros or become our first planned corpse."

Sharp muzzles jabbed into my back. "But Ragin—I'm a physical, not a mucilaginous chemist. Do you know what viscodium is? There's a joke in the student labs: what viscodium hath joined together, no man can put asunder. It takes on the physical properties of whatever it congeals around and dendraloid is the hardest substance in the galaxy. If you try to split the block, you split the Dendros, too. The manufacturers are still working on a softener.

They warn people not to use the stuff unless they intend it to be permanent."

"Well, Dr. Sims, you better start inventing," the leader said over his shoulder. He paused at the exit hatch. "You have exactly three weeks, figuring on Terran time."

"No! Why don't you tell me the unit of liquid measure is the Sirian drom? Something I don't know, I mean." I wasn't being sarcastic; I was scared.

Three weeks to solve a problem that had the best men defeated. No lab and no equipment. And me, a neutronium specialist!

"Run down to the medicine chest and see if there's any scaralx aboard," I told one of my guards. It had proven effective in treatment of people suffering from viscodium cancer, the result of a liquid drop touching the skin.

The man tore out of the engine room. I found a morose satisfaction in the discovery that I would get cooperation.

He came back with a container of scaralx which said in large letters: DANGER! THIS COMPOUND IS TO BE TAKEN ONLY AS THE PHYSICIAN PRESCRIBES! DO NOT USE INTERNALLY.

I opened the container feverishly. There were five aspirin tablets and an eye-dropper inside.

Four days later, Ragin looked in on me on his daily tour of inspection. I had gotten around to using banked thermons. My eyes were red with fatigue. They let me go to my cabin whenever I wanted, but I hadn't been able to sleep. I was going to solve this problem and get to Earth in one piece, or I was going to burst my frontal lobe.

"How's it going, doc?" the big man asked.

"Not so good," I grunted. "I don't dare use too much juice for fear of melting the machinery. I've been trying to run it on an alternating current generator so that the heat is applied only to the surface in short bursts. But this stuff conducts too damn fast. I'll solve it somehow, though."

"Attaboy," he encouraged. "That's the old scientific spirit."

He wilted under my glare. "Sorry. I've no call to be funny. I wish those slobs—Steggo and Skandelli—were here. They'd have their mouths washed with viscodium, they would. Although," he considered, "they probably despise us just as much as we do them. You're the only innocent bystander."

The women, dressed in gay Aldebaranian frocks, were peering anxiously through the hatch. I thought of how much workable Dendros meant to them. After all, their claim was as just as mine.

"Forget it."

"You see," he explained anxiously, "this is a democracy we have here, a democracy of the purest kind because it's still close to the conditions which produced it. I'm only the leader; and even if I wanted to set you free because I trust you, the rest of the men can't feel that sure."

"I understand. You have a sound mind, Ragin. A pity only Solarians and Sagittarians are allowed in galactic government."

"Yeah. That's what I kept telling them."

Everybody laughed and tension dissolved. Gonda leaned over his shmobber and said to a neighbor: "See, what did I tell you—the doc *is* a good guy!

The tall mutineer came over and stood at my side. Together we stared at the stubborn viscodium, green and immovable.

We all perspired quietly in useless, repetitious thought.

"It beats the living shavings out of me," Ragin said finally, "how that goo won't let us make any adjustments in the Dendros that will turn us away from the Solarian Patrol, but keeps them working the way they were set."

"Property of the substance," I yawned wearily. "In order to steer you must use the Dendros as moving parts; viscodium between the parts precludes that. However,

Dendros merely vibrate through the space warp on straight drive; the viscodium having assumed the characteristics of the substance to which it adheres, vibrates along with it, actually adding to its efficiency. If the Dendros stop, so does the viscodium. Any activity of the bound object automatically becomes an activity of that filthy slime."

"Suppose you change the make-up of the Dendros, then. You could negate them and take the whole business apart with hyper-tongs. After we got rid of the viscodium, the boys would reassemble the machines and make 'em solid. No?"

I shook my head. "No. Space negation is dangerous enough with the proper equipment and under the proper conditions. Here, you'd just save the Solarian Patrol a lot of grief by tearing a hole right through the ether. Besides, you can't negate dendraloid. Of course, if you could change the physical properties of dendraloid enough to pick the viscodium off, you'd be set. But any way I figure it, you wind up without any motors at all."

"And with the ship carrying no transmitter, that would not be nice. No matter what these damned bushaleons are doing to us, we have to keep them in good condition. I have the boys oiling them internally every six hours. That's the minimum period according to the manual."

When I could get my tongue disentangled from my teeth, I grabbed his arm. "Oil them? What kind of oil?"

He looked down, puzzled. "Machine oil. Not the Terran kind—"

"You poor, broken blasthead!" I yelled. "Is there any molecular joint lubricant on this filthy, meteor-broken scow?"

A light of purest joy broke over his face. He snapped out an order.

One of the men scurried to a cabinet and peered inside. At his triumphant shout everybody exhaled gustily.

"Use the mittens," I called to him. "There should be a pair of insulated mittens next to the case."

The Aldebaranian came staggering back with a container whose walls were made of thinnest neutronium. Inside it splashed the most beautiful purple liquid I'd ever seen. Molecular oil!

It meant a reprieve from the negative space foundries for the men. It meant a reprieve from imprisonment with Fino Feminists for the women. As for me—it meant reprieve. . . .

"Dig up a couple of loading pipes," I ordered. "Clean ones. They're the only things that have linings to take the stuff. You can make one of them into a funnel and cup it under the whole block of Dendros and solid viscodium. Then run a pipe from the funnel to an air lock and if it works we can pump the goo right out into space."

"If it works!" Ragin caroled. "It's got to work! We're down to our last electron in this pot. It's got to work!"

It worked.

We poured the purple liquid into a vat of Sirian machine oil. Then we squirted the mixture, at the highest pressure we could generate, along the Dendro input pipes under the floor plates. It took a while for the super lubricant to work its way through the heavy colloid. Then the outside of the machinery shone with a sudden purple sheen as oil oozed through the molecules of dendraloid.

Ragin yelled and pounded my back.

Slowly the viscodium changed from green to purple. It became softer and softer, as the physical characteristics of the object it gripped changed from solid to liquid. Finally, it flowed evenly into the funnel. We heard it gurgling through the loading pipe on the way to the air lock, moving slower and becoming more viscous as it went.

One of the mutineers volunteered to crawl under the Dendros. While we watched breathlessly, he held the neutronium container under the tapering, bottom point of the drive motors. He caught every drop of the molecular joint lubricant in the container. Naturally—he had to.

Ballew turned from his charts and said, "I hope you won't get angry, but the men are—well, insistent that you stay in your cabin while the lifeboats are leaving. It isn't that they don't trust you, but—"

"They feel my conscience will help my mouth in depriving the Solarian Patrol of information if I don't know where they're heading. I understand."

He smiled at me out of poor teeth. "That's it. While you were prying the viscodium loose, I was a prisoner in the bridge. And I've known these men for years. They felt that as an officer, I didn't have the same size stake as say Ragin has, with his wife involved the way she is. They were right. That's why I'm staying aboard with you. I'm going on to Sol."

"Are you that confident I won't inform on you?"

A rustle of charts as he turned one around. There was a youthful grin on his face. "Yes. You see we had your cabin searched before the mutiny. Nothing important was found. Except for half a container of *unused* depilosac dissolving in the waste chamber."

I stopped breathing and sat up straight. What a stupid slip!

"Ragin claimed it meant nothing. I didn't think so. I thought about it and thought about it until I came to the one possible solution. Now I know you have just as much interest in my not talking about this trip as I have in your keeping quiet. So I'm going on to Sol and after the patrol finishes its routine check—it won't be more than that with Ragin taking all responsibility in the log—I'll go my way and you'll go yours, *Doctor* Sims."

"Have you told anyone else?"

"Only Ragin, just after you finished with that mess in the engine room. He didn't believe it at first."

I bounded out of the room. Ragin was in his cabin with his wife. They were packing.

When I entered, he was almost halfway through the ninety-five volumes of the *Encyclopaedia Galactica*. As each volume passed into the force field of the collapsicon, it diminished to one-twentieth of its original size. I stared at the miniature books lying at the bottom of the mechanical valise.

The Aldebaranian woman left quietly in response to her husband's signal. I cleared my throat. "Don't open that thing suddenly when you start unpacking, or you'll think an avalanche hit you."

He shifted uncomfortably. "I know. I've used collapsicons before." There was a silence.

"And how do you expect to live on a bare planetoid? You can't grow food where there isn't oxygen."

"Oh, we sunk our money in extractors. We'll be able to suck enough raw elements out of whatever we hit to get started. After that it's a matter of our own ingenuity."

"And the books are for your children?"

"Yeah. Elsa wants a lot of them. And I'm going to see they grow up with all the knowledge the galaxy has available."

Ragin coughed. "By the Hole in Cygnus, doctor, why couldn't you wait? A naval employee, too! Six months and the liners would be running again, and everything would be open and above-board."

"I have a son in a naval hospital on Earth," I told him. "We haven't seen each other in three years and I still couldn't get a priority. He may be dead in six months."

"Yes, that would be it. But your papers—"

"My papers refer to Dr. R. Sims, physical chemist, of naval research, Aldebaranian Project CBX-19329. Horkey, my superior, made them out for me just that way, gave me an indefinite leave of absence, and wished me luck."

He squeezed my hand in a last, friendly mangle and

accompanied me to the door. "Don't worry about Ballew. He's a good kid. The only reason he mentioned his discovery at all was because he decided to go to Sol and he wanted you to know how secure he felt. He's read too many books, maybe."

Before they left, the mutineers showed Ballew and me how to set the Dendros. In the end, he worked out the charts and I tended the machinery. Just as well. I felt safer that way.

"You know," Ballew said lazily as he waited for the Solarian warpers to pull us into the system. "All I can think of is a little old bar in New York. A little old bar where I'm going to get stinking drunk."

He was cute. Personally, I was dreaming of Max's Salon in Chicago. Max's where I, Roberta Sims, Sc. D., Ph. D., Ga. D., would be getting a glorious terrestrial permanent wave.

After my hair had grown back, of course.

■ VENUS IS A MAN'S WORLD ■

I'VE ALWAYS said that even if Sis is seven years older than me—and a girl besides—she don't always know what's best. Put me on a spaceship jam-packed with three hundred females just aching to get themselves husbands in the one place they're still to be had—the planet Venus— and you know I'll be in trouble.

Bad trouble. With the law, which is the worst a boy can get into.

Twenty minutes after we lifted from the Sahara Spaceport, I wriggled out of my acceleration hammock and started for the door of our cabin.

"Now you be careful, Ferdinand," Sis called after me as she opened a book called *Family Problems of the Frontier Woman*. "Remember you're a nice boy. Don't make me ashamed of you."

I tore down the corridor. Most of the cabins had purple lights on in front of the doors, showing that the girls were still inside their hammocks. That meant only the ship's crew was up and about. Ship's crews are men; women are too busy with important things like government to run ships. I felt free all over—and happy. Now was my chance to really see the *Eleanor Roosevelt!*

It was hard to believe I was traveling in space at last. Ahead and behind me, all the way up to where the companionway curved in out of sight, there was nothing but smooth black wall and smooth white doors—on and on and on. *Gee,* I thought excitedly, *this is one big ship!*

Of course, every once in a while I would run across a big scene of stars in the void set in the wall; but they were only pictures. Nothing that gave the feel of great empty space like I'd read about in *The Boy Rocketeers,* no portholes, no visiplates, nothing.

So when I came to the crossway, I stopped for a second, then turned left. To the right, see, there was Deck Four, then Deck Three, leading inward past the engine fo'c'sle to the main jets and the grav helix going *purr-purr-purrty-purr* in the comforting way big machinery has when it's happy and oiled. But to the left, the crossway led all the way to the outside level which ran just under the hull. There were portholes on the hull.

I'd studied all that out in our cabin, long before we'd lifted, on the transparent model of the ship hanging like a big cigar from the ceiling. Sis had studied it too, but she was looking for places like the dining salon and the library and Lifeboat 68 where we should go in case of emergency. I looked for the *important* things.

As I trotted along the crossway, I sort of wished that Sis hadn't decided to go after a husband on a luxury liner. On a cargo ship, now, I'd be climbing from deck to deck on a ladder instead of having gravity underfoot all the time just like I was home on the bottom of the Gulf of Mexico. But women always know what's right, and a boy can only make faces and do what they say, same as the men have to do.

Still, it was pretty exciting to press my nose against the slots in the wall and see the sliding panels that could come charging out and block the crossway into an airtight fit in case a meteor or something smashed into the ship. And all along there were glass cases with spacesuits standing in them, like those knights they used to have back in the Middle Ages.

"In the event of disaster affecting the oxygen content of companionway," they had the words etched into the glass, "break glass with hammer upon wall, remove spacesuit and proceed to don it in the following fashion."

I read the "following fashion" until I knew it by heart. *Boy,* I said to myself, *I hope we have that kind of disaster. I'd sure like to get into one of those! Bet it would be more fun than those diving suits back in Undersea!*

And all the time I was alone. That was the best part.

Then I passed Deck Twelve and there was a big sign. "Notice! Passengers not permitted past this point!" A big sign in red.

I peeked around the corner. I knew it—the next deck was the hull. I could see the portholes. Every twelve feet, they were, filled with the velvet of space and the dancing of more stars than I'd ever dreamed existed in the Universe.

There wasn't anyone on the deck, as far as I could see. And this distance from the grav helix, the ship seemed mighty quiet and lonely. If I just took one quick look . . .

But I thought of what Sis would say and I turned around obediently. Then I saw the big red sign again. "Passengers not permitted—"

Well! Didn't I know from my civics class that only women could be Earth Citizens these days? Sure, ever since the Male Desuffrage Act. And didn't I know that you had to be a citizen of a planet in order to get an interplanetary passport? Sis had explained it all to me in the careful, patient way she always talks politics and things like that to men.

"Technically, Ferdinand, I'm the only passenger in our family. You can't be one, because, not being a citizen, you can't acquire an Earth Passport. However, you'll be going to Venus on the strength of this clause—"Miss Evelyn

Sparling and all dependent male members of family, this number not to exceed the registered quota of sub-regulations pertaining'—and so on. I want you to understand these matters, so that you will grow into a man who takes an active interest in world affairs. No matter what you hear, women really like and appreciate such men."

Of course, I never pay much attention to Sis when she says such dumb things. I'm old enough, I guess, to know that it isn't what *women* like and appreciate that counts when it comes to people getting married. If it were, Sis and three hundred other pretty girls like her wouldn't be on their way to Venus to hook husbands.

Still, if I wasn't a passenger, the sign didn't have anything to do with me. I knew what Sis could say to *that*, but at least it was an argument I could use if it ever came up. So I broke the law.

I was glad I did. The stars were exciting enough, but away off to the left, about five times as big as I'd ever seen it, except in the movies, was the Moon, a great blob of gray and white pockmarks holding off the black of space. I was hoping to see the Earth, but I figured it must be on the other side of the ship or behind us. I pressed my nose against the port and saw the tiny flicker of a spaceliner taking off, Marsbound. I wished I was on that one!

Then I noticed, a little farther down the companion-way, a stretch of blank wall where there should have been portholes. High up on the wall in glowing red letters were the words, "Lifeboat 47. Passengers: Thirty-two. Crew: Eleven. Unauthorized personnel keep away!"

Another one of those signs.

I crept up to the porthole nearest it and could just barely make out the stern jets where they were jammed against the hull. Then I walked under the sign and tried to figure the way you were supposed to get into it. There was a very thin line going around in a big circle that I knew must be the door. But I couldn't see any knobs or switches to open it with. Not even a button you could press.

That meant it was a sonic lock like the kind we had on the outer keeps back home in Undersea. But knock or voice? I tried the two knock combinations I knew, and nothing happened. I only remembered one voice key— might as well see if that's it, I figured.

"Twenty, Twenty-three. Open Sesame."

For a second, I thought I'd hit it just right out of all the million possible combinations— The door clicked inward toward a black hole, and a hairy hand as broad as my shoulders shot out of the hole. It closed around my throat and plucked me inside as if I'd been a baby sardine.

I bounced once on the hard lifeboat floor. Before I got my breath and sat up, the door had been shut again. When the light came on, I found myself staring up the muzzle of a highly polished blaster and into the cold blue eyes of the biggest man I'd ever seen.

He was wearing a one-piece suit made of some scaly green stuff that looked hard and soft at the same time.

His boots were made of it too, and so was the hood hanging down his back.

And his face was brown. Not just ordinary tan, you understand, but the deep, dark, burned-all-the-way-in brown I'd been on the life guards in New Orleans whenever we took a surface vacation—the kind of tan that comes from day after broiling day under a really hot sun. His hair looked as if it had once been blond, but now there were just long combed-out waves with a yellowish tinge that boiled all the way down to his shoulders.

I hadn't seen hair like that on a man except maybe in history books; every man I'd ever known had his hair cropped in the fashionable soup-bowl style. I was staring at his hair, almost forgetting about the blaster which I knew it was against the law for him to have at all, when I suddenly got scared right through.

His eyes.

They didn't blink and there seemed to be no expression around them. Just coldness. Maybe it was the kind of clothes he was wearing that did it, but all of a sudden I was reminded of a crocodile I'd seen in a surface zoo that had stared quietly at me for twenty minutes until it opened two long tooth-studded jaws.

"Green shatas!" he said suddenly. "Only a tadpole. I must be getting jumpy enough to splash."

Then he shoved the blaster away in a holster made of the same scaly leather, crossed his arms on his chest and began to study me. I grunted to my feet, feeling a lot better. The coldness had gone out of his eyes.

I held out my hand the way Sis had taught me. "My name is Ferdinand Sparling. I'm very pleased to meet you, Mr.—Mr.—"

"Hope for your sake," he said to me, "that you aren't what you seem—tadpole brother to one of them husband-less anura."

"What?"

"A 'nuran is a female looking to nest. Anura is a herd of same. Come from Flatfolk ways."

"Flatfolk are the Venusian natives, aren't they? Are you a Venusian? What part of Venus do you come from? Why did you say you hope—"

He chuckled and swung me up into one of the bunks that lined the lifeboat. "Questions you ask," he said in his soft voice. "Venus is a sharp enough place for a dryhorn, let alone a tadpole dryhorn with a boss-minded sister."

"I'm not a dryleg," I told him proudly. *"We're* from Undersea."

"Dry*horn*, I said, not dryleg. And what's Undersea?"

"Well, in Undersea we called foreigners and newcomers drylegs. Just like on Venus, I guess, you call them dryhorns." And then I told him how Undersea had been built on the bottom of the Gulf of Mexico, when the mineral resources of the land began to give out and engineers figured that a lot could still be reached from the sea bottoms.

He nodded. He'd heard about the sea-bottom mining cities that were bubbling under protective domes in every one of the Earth's oceans just about the same time settlements were springing up on the planets.

He looked impressed when I told him about Mom and Pop being one of the first couples to get married in Undersea. He looked thoughtful when I told him how Sis and I had been born there and spent half our childhood listening to the pressure pumps. He raised his eyebrows and looked disgusted when I told how Mom, as Undersea representative on the World Council, had been one of the framers of the Male Desuffrage Act after the Third Atomic War had resulted in the Maternal Revolution.

And then he punched my arm when I got to the time Mom and Pop were blown up in a surfacing boat.

"Well, after the funeral, there was a little money, so Sis decided we might as well use it to migrate. There was no future for her on Earth, she figured. You know, the three-out-of-four."

"How's that?"

"The three-out-of-four. No more than three women out of every four on Earth can expect to find husbands. Not enough men to go around. Way back in the twentieth century, it began to be felt, Sis says, what with the wars and all. Then the wars went on and a lot more men began to die or get no good from the radioactivity. Then the best men went to the planets, Sis says, until by now even if a woman can scrounge a personal husband, he's not much to boast about."

The stranger nodded violently. "Not on Earth, he isn't. Those busybody anura make sure of that. What a place! Suffering gridniks, I had a bellyful!"

He told me about it. Women were scarce on Venus, and

he hadn't been able to find any who were willing to come out to his lonely little islands; he had decided to go to Earth where there was supposed to be a surplus. Naturally, having been born and brought up on a very primitive planet, he didn't know "it's a woman's world," like the older boys in school used to say.

The moment he landed on Earth he was in trouble. He didn't know he had to register at a government-operated hotel for transient males; he threw a bartender through a thick plastic window for saying something nasty about the length of his hair; and *imagine!*—he not only resisted arrest, resulting in three hospitalized policemen, but he sassed the judge in open court!

"Told me a man wasn't supposed to say anything except through female attorneys. Told *her* that where *I* came from, a man spoke his piece when he'd a mind to, and his woman walked by his side."

"What happened?" I asked breathlessly.

"Oh, Guilty of This and Contempt of That. That blown-up brinosaur took my last munit for fines, then explained that she was remitting the rest because I was a foreigner and uneducated." His eyes grew dark for a moment. He chuckled again. "But I wasn't going to serve all those fancy little prison sentences. Forcible Citizenship Indoctrination, they call it? Shook the dead-dry dust of the misbegotten, God-forsaken mother world from my feet forever. The women on it deserve their men. My pockets were folded from the fines, and the paddlefeet were looking for me so close I didn't dare radio for more munit. So I stowed away."

For a moment, I didn't understand him. When I did, I was almost ill. "Y-you mean," I choked, "th-that you're b-breaking the law right now? And I'm with you while you're doing it?"

He leaned over the edge of the bunk and stared at me very seriously. "What breed of tadpole are they turning out these days? Besides, what business do *you* have this close to the hull?"

After a moment of sober reflection, I nodded. "You're right. I've also become a male outside the law. We're in this together."

He guffawed. Then he sat up and began cleaning his blaster. I found myself drawn to the bright killer-tube with exactly the fascination Sis insists such things have always had for men.

"Ferdinand your label? That's not right for a sprouting tadpole. I'll call you Ford. My name's Butt. Butt Lee Brown."

I liked the sound of Ford. "Is Butt a nickname, too?"

"Yeah. Short for Alberta, but I haven't found a man who can draw a blaster fast enough to call me that. You see, Pop came over in the eighties—the big wave of immigrants when they evacuated Ontario. Named all us boys after Canadian provinces. I was the youngest, so I got the name they were saving for a girl."

"You had a lot of brothers, Mr. Butt?"

He grinned with a mighty set of teeth. "Oh, a nestful. Of course, they were all killed in the Blue Chicago Rising by the MacGregor boys—all except me and Saskatchewan. Then Sas and me hunted the MacGregors down. Took a heap of time; we ,didn't float Jock MacGregor's ugly face down the Tuscany till both of us were pretty near grown up."

I walked up close to where I could see the tiny bright copper coils of the blaster above the firing button. "Have you killed a lot of men with that, Mr. Butt?"

"Butt. Just plain Butt to you, Ford." He frowned and sighted at the light globe. "No more'n twelve—not counting five government paddlefeet, of course. I'm a peaceable planter. Way I figure it, violence never accomplishes much that's important. My brother Sas, now—"

He had just begun to work into this wonderful story about his brother when the dinner gong rang. Butt told me to scat. He said I was a growing tadpole and needed my vitamins. And he mentioned, very off-hand, that he wouldn't at all object if I brought him some fresh fruit. It seemed there was nothing but processed foods in the lifeboat and Butt was used to a farmer's diet.

Trouble was, he was a special kind of farmer. Ordinary fruit would have been pretty easy to sneak into my pockets at meals. I even found a way to handle the kelp and giant watercress Mr. Brown liked, but things like seaweed salt and Venusian mudgrapes just had too strong a smell. Twice, the mechanical hamper refused to accept my jacket for laundering and I had to wash it myself. But I learned so many wonderful things about Venus every time I visited that stowaway . . .

I learned three wild-wave songs of the Flatfolk and what it is that the native Venusians hate so much; I learned how you tell the difference between a lousy government paddlefoot from New Kalamazoo and the slaptoe slinker who is the planter's friend. After a lot of begging, Butt Lee Brown explained the workings of his blaster, explained it so carefully that I could name every part and tell what it did from the tiny round electrodes to the long spirals of transformer. But no matter what, he would never let me hold it.

"Sorry, Ford, old tad," he would drawl, spinning around and around in the control swivel-chair at the nose of the lifeboat. "But way I look at it, a man who lets somebody else handle his blaster is like the giant whose heart was in an egg that an enemy found. When you've grown enough so's your pop feels you ought to have a weapon, why, then's the time to learn it and you might's well learn fast. Before then, you're plain too young to be even near it."

"I don't have a father to give me one when I come of

age. I don't even have an older brother as head of my family like your brother Labrador. All I have is Sis. And *she—*"

"She'll marry some fancy dryhorn who's never been farther South than the Polar Coast. And she'll stay head of the family, if I know her breed of green shata. *Bossy, opinionated.* By the way, Fordie," he said, rising and stretching so the fish-leather bounced and rippled off his biceps, "that sister. She ever . . ."

And he'd be off again, cross-examining me about Evelyn. I sat in the swivel chair he'd vacated and tried to answer his questions. But there was a lot of stuff I didn't know. Evelyn was a healthy girl, for instance; how healthy, exactly, I had no way of finding out. Yes, I'd tell him, my aunts on both sides of my family had each had more than the average number of children. No, we'd never done any farming to speak of, back in Undersea, but— yes, I'd guess Evelyn knew about as much as any girl there when it came to diving equipment and pressure pump regulation.

How would I know that stuff would lead to trouble for me?

Sis had insisted I come along to the geography lecture. Most of the other girls who were going to Venus for husbands talked to each other during the lecture, but not *my* sister! She hung on every word, took notes even, and asked enough questions to make the perspiring purser really work in those orientation periods.

"I am very sorry, Miss Sparling," he said with pretty heavy sarcasm, "but I cannot remember any of the agricultural products of the Macro Continent. Since the human population is well below one per thousand square miles, it can readily be understood that the quantity of tilled soil, land or sub-surface, is so small that— Wait, I remember something. The Macro Continent exports a fruit though not exactly an edible one. The wild *dunging* drug is harvested there by criminal speculators. Contrary to belief on Earth, the traffic has been growing in recent years. In fact—"

"Pardon me, sir," I broke in, "but doesn't *dunging* come only from Leif Erickson Island off the Moscow Peninsula of the Macro Continent? You remember, purser—Wang Li's third exploration, where he proved the island and the peninsula didn't meet for most of the year?"

The purser nodded slowly. "I forgot," he admitted. "Sorry, ladies, but the boy's right. Please make the correction in your notes."

But Sis was the only one who took notes, and she didn't take that one. She stared at me for a moment, biting her lower lip thoughtfully, while I got sicker and sicker. Then she shut her pad with the final gesture of the right hand that Mom used to use just before challenging the opposition to come right down on the Council floor and debate it out with her.

"Ferdinand," Sis said, "let's go back to our cabin."

The moment she sat me down and walked slowly around me, I knew I was in for it. "I've been reading up on Venusian geography in the ship's library," I told her in a hurry.

"No doubt," she said drily. She shook her night-black hair out. "But you aren't going to tell me that you read about *dunging* in the ship's library. The books there have been censored by a government agent of Earth against the possibility that they might be read by susceptible young male minds like yours. She would not have allowed—this Terran Agent—"

"Paddlefoot," I sneered.

Sis sat down hard in our zoom-air chair. "Now that's a term," she said carefully, "that is used only by Venusian riffraff."

"They're not!"

"Not what?"

"Riffraff," I had to answer, knowing I was getting in deeper all the time and not being able to help it. I mustn't give Mr. Brown away! "They're trappers and farmers, pioneers and explorers, who're building Venus. And it takes a real man to build on a hot, hungry hell like Venus."

"Does it now?" she said, looking at me as if I were beginning to grow a second pair of ears. "Tell me more."

"You can't have meek, law-abiding, women-ruled men when you start civilization on a new planet. You've got to have men who aren't afraid to make their own law if necessary—with their own guns. That's where law begins; the books get written up later."

"You're going to *tell,* Ferdinand, what evil, criminal male is speaking through your mouth!"

"Nobody!" I insisted. "They're my own ideas!"

"They are remarkably well-organized for a young boy's ideas. A boy who, I might add, has previously shown a ridiculous but nonetheless entirely masculine boredom with political philosophy. I plan to have a government career on that new planet you talk about, Ferdinand— after I have found a good, steady husband, of course— and I don't look forward to a masculinist radical in the family. Now, who has been filling your head with all this nonsense?"

I was sweating. Sis has that deadly bulldog approach when she feels someone is lying. I began to pull my handkerchief from my pocket to wipe my face. Something rattled to the floor.

"What is this picture of me doing in your pocket, Ferdinand?"

A trap seemed to be banging noisily into place. "One of the passengers wanted to see how you looked in a bathing suit."

"The passengers on this ship are all female. I can't imagine any of them that curious about my appearance.

Ferdinand, it's a man who has been giving you these antisocial ideas, isn't it? A war-mongering masculinist like all the frustrated men who want to engage in government and don't have the vaguest idea of how. Except, of course, in their ancient, bloody ways. Ferdinand, who has been perverting that sunny and carefree soul of yours?"

"Nobody! *Nobody!*"

"Ferdinand, there's no point in lying! I demand——"

"I told you, Sis. I told you! And don't call me Ferdinand. Call me Ford."

"Ford? *Ford?* Now, you listen to me, Ferdinand . . ."

After that it was all over but the confession. That came in a few moments. I couldn't fool Sis. She just knew me too well, I decided miserably. Besides, she was a girl.

All the same, I wouldn't get Mr. Butt Lee Brown into trouble if I could help it. I made Sis promise she wouldn't turn him in if I took her to him. And the quick, nodding way she said she would made me feel just a little better.

The door opened on the signal, "Sesame." When Butt saw somebody was with me, he jumped and the ten-inch blaster barrel grew out of his fingers. Then he recognized Sis from the pictures.

He stepped to one side and, with the same sweeping gesture, holstered his blaster and pushed his green hood off. It was Sis's turn to jump when she saw the wild mass of hair rolling down his back.

"An honor, Miss Sparling," he said in that rumbly voice. "Please come right in. There's a hurry-up draft."

So Sis went in and I followed right after her. Mr. Brown closed the door. I tried to catch his eye so I could give him some kind of hint or explanation, but he had taken a couple of his big strides and was in the forward section with Sis. She didn't give ground, though; I'll say that for her. She only came to his chest, but she had her arms crossed sternly.

"First, Mr. Brown," she began, like talking to a cluck

of a kid in class, "you realize that you are not only committing the political crime of traveling without a visa, and the clear felony of stowing away without paying your fare, but the moral delinquency of consuming stores intended for the personnel of this ship solely in emergency?"

He opened his mouth to its maximum width and raised an enormous hand. Then he let the air out and dropped his arm.

"I take it you either have no defense or care to make none," Sis added caustically.

Butt laughed slowly and carefully as if he were going over each word. "Wonder if all the anura talk like that. And *you* want to foul up Venus."

"We haven't done so badly on Earth, after the mess you men made of politics. It needed a revolution of the mothers before—"

"Needed nothing. Everyone wanted peace. Earth is a weary old world."

"It's a world of strong moral fiber compared to yours, Mr. Alberta Lee Brown." Hearing his rightful name made him move suddenly and tower over her. Sis said with a certain amount of hurry and change of tone, "What *do* you have to say about stowing away and using up lifeboat stores?"

He cocked his head and considered a moment. "Look," he said finally, "I have more than enough munit to pay for round trip tickets, but I couldn't get a return visa because of that brinosaur judge and all the charges she hung on me. Had to stow away. Picked the *Eleanor Roosevelt* because a couple of the boys in the crew are friends of mine and they were willing to help. But this lifeboat—don't you know that every passenger ship carries four times as many lifeboats as it needs? Not to mention the food I didn't eat because it stuck in my throat?"

"Yes," she said bitterly. "You had this boy steal fresh

fruit for you. I suppose you didn't know that under space regulations that makes him equally guilty?"

"No, Sis, he didn't," I was beginning to argue. "All he wanted—"

"Sure I knew. Also know that if I'm picked up as a stowaway, I'll be sent back to Earth to serve out those fancy little sentences."

"Well, you're guilty of them, aren't you?"

He waved his hands at her impatiently. "I'm not talking law, female; I'm talking sense. Listen! I'm in trouble because I went to Earth to look for a wife. You're standing here right now because you're on your way to Venus for a husband. So let's."

Sis actually staggered back. "Let's? Let's *what?* Are—are you daring to suggest that—that—"

"Now, Miss Sparling, no hoopla. I'm saying let's get married, and you know it. You figured out from what the boy told you that I was chewing on you for a wife. You're healthy and strong, got good heredity, you know how to operate sub-surface machinery, you've lived underwater, and your disposition's no worse than most of the anura I've seen. Prolific stock, too."

I was so excited I just had to yell: "Gee, Sis, say *yes!*"

My sister's voice was steaming with scorn. "And what makes you think that I'd consider you a desirable husband?"

He spread his hands genially. "Figure if you wanted a poodle, you're pretty enough to pick one up on Earth. Figure if you charge off to Venus, you don't want a poodle, you want a man. I'm one. I own three islands in the Galertan Archipelago that'll be good oozing mudgrape land when they're cleared. Not to mention the rich berzeliot beds offshore. I got no bad habits outside of having my own way. I'm also passable good-looking for a slaptoe planter. Besides, if you marry me you'll be the first mated on this ship—and that's a splash most nesting females like to make."

There was a longish stretch of quiet. Sis stepped back and measured him slowly with her eyes; there was a lot to look at. He waited patiently while she covered the distance from his peculiar green boots to that head of hair. I was so excited I was gulping instead of breathing. Imagine having Butt for a brother-in-law and living on a wet-plantation in Flatfolk country!

But then I remembered Sis's level head and I didn't have much hope any more.

"You know," she began, "there's more to marriage than just—"

"So there is," he cut in. "Well, we can try each other for taste." And he pulled her in, both of his great hands practically covering her slim, straight back.

Neither of them said anything for a bit after he let go. Butt spoke up first.

"Now, me," he said, "I'd vote yes."

Sis ran the tip of her tongue kind of delicately from side to side of her mouth. Then she moved back thinking and looked at him as if she were figuring out how many feet high he was. She kept on moving backward, tapping her chin, while Butt and I got more and more impatient. When she touched the lifeboat door, she pushed it open and jumped out.

Butt ran over and looked down the crossway. After a while, he shut the door and came back beside me. "Well," he said, swinging to a bunk, "that's sort of it."

"You're better off, Butt," I burst out. "You shouldn't have a woman like Sis for a wife. She looks small and helpless, but don't forget she was trained to run an underwater city!"

"Wasn't worrying about that," he grinned. "*I* grew up in the fifteen long years of the Blue Chicago Rising.

Nope." He turned over on his back and clicked his teeth at the ceiling. "Think we'd have nested out nicely."

I hitched myself up to him and we sat on the bunk, glooming away at each other. Then we heard the tramp of feet in the crossway.

Butt swung down and headed for the control compartment in the nose of the lifeboat. He had his blaster out and was cursing very interestingly. I started after him, but he picked me up by the seat of my jumper and tossed me toward the door. The Captain came in and tripped over me.

I got all tangled up in his gold braid and million-mile space buttons. When we finally got to our feet and sorted out right, he was breathing very hard. The Captain was a round little man with a plump, golden face and a very scared look on it. He *humphed* at me, just the way Sis does, and lifted me by the scruff of my neck. The Chief Mate picked me up and passed me to the Second Assistant Engineer.

Sis was there, being held by the purser on one side and the Chief Computer's Mate on the other. Behind them, I could see a flock of wide-eyed female passengers.

"You cowards!" Sis was raging. "Letting your captain face a dangerous outlaw all by himself!"

"I dunno, Miss Sparling," the Computer's Mate said, scratching the miniature slide-rule insignia on his visor with his free hand. "The Old Man would've been willing to let it go with a log entry, figuring the spaceport paddle-feet could pry out the stowaway when we landed. But you had to quote the Mother Anita Law at him, and he's in there doing his duty. He figures the rest of us are family men, too, and there's no sense making orphans."

"You promised, Sis," I told her through my teeth. "You promised you wouldn't get Butt into trouble!"

She tossed her spiral curls at me and ground a heel into

the purser's instep. He screwed up his face and howled, but he didn't let go of her arm.

"*Shush*, Ferdinand, this is serious!"

It was. I heard the Captain say, "I'm not carrying a weapon, Brown."

"Then *get* one," Butt's low, lazy voice floated out.

"No, thanks. You're as handy with that thing as I am with a rocketboard." The Captain's words got a little fainter as he walked forward. Butt growled like a gusher about to blow.

"I'm counting on your being a good guy, Brown." The Captain's voice quavered just a bit. "I'm banking on what I heard about the blast-happy Browns every time I lifted gravs in New Kalamazoo; they have a code, they don't burn unarmed men."

Just about this time, events in the lifeboat went down to a mumble. The top of my head got wet and I looked up. There was sweat rolling down the Second Assistant's forehead; it converged at his nose and bounced off the tip in a thin little stream. I twisted out of the way.

"What's happening?" Sis gritted, straining toward the lock.

"Butt's trying to decide whether he wants him fried or scrambled," the Computer's Mate said, pulling her back. "Hey, purse, remember when the whole family with their pop at the head went into Heatwave to argue with Colonel Leclerc?"

"Eleven dead, sixty-four injured," the purser answered mechanically. "And no more army stationed south of Icebox." His right ear twitched irritably. "But what're they saying?"

Suddenly we heard. "By authority vested in me under the Pomona College Treaty," the Captain was saying very loudly, "I arrest you for violation of Articles Sixteen to Twenty-one inclusive of the Space Transport Code, and order your person and belongings impounded for the dur-

ation of this voyage as set forth in Sections Forty-one and
Forty-five—"

"Forty-three and Forty-five," Sis groaned. "Sections
Forty-three and Forty-five, I told him. I even made him
repeat it after me!"

"—of the Mother Anita Law, SC 2136, Emergency
Interplanetary Directives."

We all waited breathlessly for Butt's reply. The seconds
ambled on and there was no clatter of electrostatic dis-
charge, no smell of burning flesh.

Then we heard some feet walking. A big man in a
green suit swung out into the crossway. That was Butt.
Behind him came the Captain, holding the blaster gingerly
with both hands. Butt had a funny, thoughtful look on his
face.

The girls surged forward when they saw him, scattering
the crew to one side. They were like a school of sharks
that had just caught sight of a dying whale.

"M-m-m-m! Are all Venusians built like that?"

"Men like that are worth the mileage!"

"I want him!" "I want him!" "I want him!"

Sis had been let go. She grabbed my free hand and
pulled me away. She was trying to look only annoyed, but
her eyes had bright little bubbles of fury popping in them.

"The cheap extroverts! And they call themselves responsible women!"

I was angry, too. And I let her know, once we were in
our cabin. "What about that promise, Sis? You said you
wouldn't turn him in. You *promised!*"

She stopped walking around the room as if she had
been expecting to get to Venus on foot. "I know I did
Ferdinand, but he forced me."

"My name is Ford and I don't understand."

"Your name is Ferdinand and stop trying to act force-
fully like a girl. It doesn't become you. In just a few days,
you'll forget all this and be your simple, carefree self

again. I really truly meant to keep my word. From what you'd told me, Mr. Brown seemed to be a fundamentally decent chap despite his barbaric notions on equality between the sexes—or worse. I was positive I could shame him into a more rational social behavior and make him give himself up. Then he—he—"

She pressed her fingernails into her palms and let out a long, glaring sigh at the door. "Then he kissed me! Oh, it was a good enough kiss—Mr. Brown has evidently had a varied and colorful background—but the galling idiocy of the man, trying that! I was just getting over the colossal impudence involved in *his* proposing marriage—as if *he* had to bear the children!—and was considering the offer seriously, on its merits, as one should consider *all* suggestions, when he deliberately dropped the pretense of reason. He appealed to me as most of the savage ancients appealed to their women, as an emotional machine. Throw the correct sexual switches, says this theory, and the female surrenders herself ecstatically to the doubtful and bloody murk of masculine plans."

There was a double knock on the door and the Captain walked in without waiting for an invitation. He was still holding Butt's blaster. He pointed it at me. "Get your hands up, Ferdinand Sparling," he said.

I did.

"I hereby order your detention for the duration of this voyage, for aiding and abetting a stowaway, as set forth in Sections Forty-one and Forty-five—"

"Forty-three and Forty-five," Sis interrupted him, her eyes getting larger and rounder. "But you gave me your word of honor that no charges would be lodged against the boy!"

"Forty-one and Forty-five," he corrected her courteously, still staring fiercely at me. "I looked it up. Of the Anita Mason Law, Emergency Interplanetary Directives. That was the usual promise one makes to an informer, but I made it before I knew it was Butt Lee Brown you were talking about. I didn't want to arrest Butt Lee Brown. You forced me. So I'm breaking my promise to you, just as, I understand, you broke your promise to your brother. They'll both be picked up at New Kalamazoo Spaceport and sent Terraward for trial."

"But I used all of our money to buy passage," Sis wailed.

"And now you'll have to return with the boy. I'm sorry, Miss Sparling. But as you explained to me, a man who has been honored with an important official position should stay close to the letter of the law for the sake of other men who are trying to break down terrestrial anti-male prejudice. Of course, there's a way out."

"There is? Tell me, please?"

"Can I lower my hands a minute?" I asked.

"No, you can't, son—not according to the armed surveillance provisions of the Mother Anita Law. Miss Sparling, if you'd marry Brown—now, now, don't look at me like that!—we could let the whole matter drop. A shipboard wedding and he goes on your passport as a 'dependent male member of family,' which means, so far as the law is concerned, that he had a regulation passport from the beginning of this voyage. And once we touch Venusian soil he can contact his bank and pay for passage. On the record, no crime was ever committed. He's free, the boy's free, and you—"

"—Are married to an uncombed desperado who doesn't know enough to sit back and let a woman run things. Oh, you should be ashamed!"

The Captain shrugged and spread his arms wide.

"Perhaps I should be, but that's what comes of putting men into responsible positions, as you would say. See here, Miss Sparling, *I* didn't want to arrest Brown, and, if it's at all possible, I'd still prefer not to. The crew, officers and men, all go along with me. We may be legal residents of Earth, but our work requires us to be on Venus several times a year. We don't want to be disliked by any members of the highly irritable Brown clan or its collateral branches. Butt Lee Brown himself, for all of his savage appearance in your civilized eyes, is a man of much influence on the Polar Continent. In his own bailiwick, the Galertan Archipelago, he makes, breaks and occasionally readjusts officials. Then there's his brother Saskatchewan who considers Butt a helpless, put-upon youngster—"

"Much influence, you say? Mr. Brown has?" Sis was suddenly thoughtful.

"Power, actually. The kind a strong man usually holds in a newly settled community. Besides, Miss Sparling, you're going to Venus for a husband because the male-female ratio on Earth is reversed. Well, not only is Butt Lee Brown a first class catch, but you can't afford to be too particular in any case. While you're fairly pretty, you won't bring any wealth into a marriage and your high degree of opinionation is not likely to be well-received on a backward, masculinist world. Then, too, the woman-hunger is not so great any more, what with the *Marie Curie* and the *Fatima* having already deposited their cargoes, the *Mme. Sun Yat Sen* due to arrive next month . . ."

Sis nodded to herself, waved the door open, and walked out.

"Let's hope," the Captain said. "Like my father used to say, a man who knows how to handle women, how to get around them without their knowing it, doesn't need to know anything else in this life. I'm plain wasted in space. You can lower your hands now, son."

We sat down and I explained the blaster to him. He was very interested. He said all Butt had told him—in the lifeboat when they decided to use my arrest as a club over Sis—was to keep the safety catch all the way up against his thumb. I could see he really had been excited about carrying a lethal weapon around. He told me that back in the old days, captains—sea captains, that is—actually had the right to keep guns in their cabins all the time to put down mutinies and other things our ancestors did.

The telewall flickered, and we turned it on. Sis smiled down. "Everything's all right, Captain. Come up and marry us, please."

"What did you stick him for?" he asked. "What was the price?"

Sis's full lips went thin and hard, the way Mom's used to. Then she thought better of it and laughed. "Mr. Brown is going to see that I'm elected sheriff of the Galertan Archipelago."

"And I thought she'd settle for a county clerkship!" the Captain muttered as we spun up to the brig.

The doors were open and girls were chattering in every corner. Sis came up to the Captain to discuss arrangements. I slipped away and found Butt sitting with folded arms in a corner of the brig. He grinned at me. "Hi, tadpole. Like the splash?"

I shook my head unhappily. "Butt, why did you do it? I'd sure love to be your brother-in-law, but, gosh, you didn't have to marry Sis." I pointed at some of the bustling females. Sis was going to have three hundred bridesmaids. "Any one of them would have jumped at the chance to be your wife. And once on any woman's passport, you'd be free. Why Sis?"

"That's what the Captain said in the lifeboat. Told him same thing I'm telling you. I'm stubborn. What I like at first, I keep on liking. What I want at first, I keep on wanting until I get."

"Yes, but making Sis sheriff! And you'll have to back her up with your blaster. What'll happen to that man's world?"

"Wait'll after we nest and go out to my islands." He

raised a calloused hand, palm upwards, and sighted along the top of it at Sis's back. "She'll be the sheriff, she will. But you know, tadpole, there are two kinds of law." The big hand went up and down. "Her law. And my law."

■ **CONSULATE** ■

I SEE by the papers where Professor Fronac says that interplanetary travel will have to go through what he calls a period of incubation. He says that after reaching the Moon, we now have hit so many new problems that we must sit down and puzzle out new theories to fit them before we can build a ship that will get us to Venus or Mars.

Of course, the Army and Navy are supervising all rocket experiments these days, and the professor's remarks are censored by them. That makes his speeches hard to understand.

But you know and I know what Professor Fronac is really saying.

The Second Martian Expedition was a complete flop. Just like the First Martian Expedition and the Venusian ones. The ships came back with all the machinery working fine and all the crews grinning with health.

But they hadn't been to Mars. They couldn't make it.

The professor goes on to say how wonderful it is that science is so wonderful, because no matter how great the obstacles, the good old scientific approach will eventually overcome them. This, he claims, is the drawing of unprejudiced conclusions from all the data available.

Well, if that's what Professor Fronac really believes, he

sure didn't act like it last August when I went all the way to Arizona to tell him just what he'd been doing wrong in those latest rocket experiments. Let me tell you, even if I am only a small-town grocer and he's a big physics professor with a Nobel Prize under his belt, he had no call to threaten me with a jail sentence just because I slipped past the Army guards at the field and hid in his bedroom! I was there only because I wanted to tell him he was on the wrong track.

If it hadn't been for poor old Fatty Myers and that option on the Winthrop store which he's going to lose by Christmas, I'd have walked out on the whole business right then and kept my mouth shut. After all, it's no skin off my nose if we never go any further than the Moon. I'm happier right here on *terra firma,* and I do mean *firma.* But, if I convince scientists, maybe I'll convince Edna.

So, for the last time, Professor Fronac and anybody else who's interested—if you really want to go places in the Solar System, you have to come down here to Massachusetts. You have to take a boat out on Cassowary Cove at night, every night, and wait. I'll help if you act halfway decent—and I'm sure Fatty Myers will do what he can— but it'll still add up to a whole lot of patience. Shoin wasn't dreefed in a riz. So they say.

Fatty had just told his assistant to take charge of the gas station that evening in March and walked slowly past the Winthrop store up to my grocery window. He waited till my wife was busy with a customer; then he caught my eye and pointed at his watch.

I shucked off my apron and pulled the heavy black sweater over my head. I had my raincoat in one hand and my fishing tackle in the other, and was just tiptoeing out when Edna saw me.

She came boiling around the counter and blocked the door with her right arm. "And where do you think you're going and leaving me to do the work of two?" she asked in that special sin-chasing voice she saves for my tiptoeing moments.

"Aw, Edna!" I said, trying to work up a grin. "I told you. Fatty's bought a new thirty-foot sloop he wants me to make sure will be in shape for the tourist trade this summer. It's dangerous for one man to sail a new boat alone at night."

"It's twice as dangerous for him with you along." She glared the grin off my face. "For the past thirty years, ever since we graduated from school, one unfailing recipe for trouble has been Paul Garland and Fatty Myers doing anything together. I still haven't forgotten the time he came over to help you install the new gas heater in our basement. You were in the hospital for five weeks and the street still looks crooked."

"The flashlight went out, Edna, and Fatty just struck a match to—"

"And what about the time, Mr. Garland," Louisa Capek, the customer, hit me from behind, "that you and Mr. Myers volunteered to shingle the church roof and fell through it on top of the minister? For eight Sundays he had to deliver sermons with his back in a cast and every one of them 'answering a fool according to his folly'!"

"How were we to know the beams were rotten? We volunteered for the job."

"You're not going, and that's final," Edna came in fast with the finisher. "So you might as well get that sweater off and the apron back on and start uncrating those cans of sardines. The two of you out on Cassowary Cove at night in a sailboat might bring on anything, including a tidal wave."

I gave Fatty the high sign, and he opened the door and squeezed in just as we had agreed he'd do in case I had trouble getting away.

"Hello, Edna and Miss Capek," he said in that cheerful belly-voice of his. "Every time I see how beautiful you look, Edna, I could kick myself around town for letting Paul steal you away from me. Ready, Paul? Paul and I are going to do a spot of fishing tonight. Maybe we can bring a nice four-pound fish back to you. Do you think you could fit it into one of those pots I gave you last Christmas, hey?"

My wife cocked her head and studied him. "Well, I think I could. But you won't be out past midnight?"

"Have him back by eleven—word of honor," Fatty promised as he grabbed me and squeezed back through the doorway.

"Remember, Paul!" Edna called after me. "Eleven o'clock! And you needn't come home if you're ten minutes late!"

That's the kind of pal Fatty was. Any wonder that I knock myself out trying to get this story told where it'll do the most good? Of course, he and Edna had been kind of sweet on each other back in school and it had been nip and tuck between us which one she'd marry. No one knew till we both got drunk at Louisa Capek's birthday party that we'd settled the problem, Fatty and I, by each catching a frog out of the creek and jumping them. Mine jumped the furthest—nine and a half feet—so I got Edna. Fatty stayed single and got fatter.

While he was starting the car, Fatty asked me what I thought of the Winthrop store as a buy for nine thousand. The Winthrop store was a big radio and electrical gadget place between my grocery and Fatty's corner service station.

I told him I thought it was a good buy for nine thousand if anyone who had the money wanted such a place.

"Well, *I* want it, Paul. I just paid old man Winthrop five hundred dollars for an option until Christmas. Between what I have in the bank and a mortgage I think I can raise on my service station, I'll have the rest. It's the coming thing in the new age."

"What's the coming thing in what new age?"

"All those scientific gadgets. The Army has just announced it's established a base on the Moon and they're going to equip it with a radio transmitter. Think of it, Paul! In a little while, we'll be getting TV broadcasts from the Moon! Then, we'll be tuning in on the latest news from Mars and Venus, the latest exploration on Mercury, the latest discovery on Pluto. People will be crazy to buy the new sets they'll need to receive that distance, kids'll be fooling around with all the new gimmicks that'll be coming out because of the inventions interplanetary travel will develop."

I watched the countryside get dark as we bounced along toward the cove. "Meanwhile, we don't have interplanetary travel. All we have is the Moon, and it don't look as if we're going further. Did you read about the Second Venusian Expedition coming back after they got two million miles out? The same thing's happened to them before, and we can't seem to make Mars either."

Fatty slapped the wheel impatiently. His jalopy swerved off the road and almost hit a fence post. "So what? They keep trying, don't they? Don't forget, the Fronac Drive's only been around for two years, and all scientists agree that, with the Drive, we can eventually go anywhere in the Solar System—maybe even to the stars after a while. It's just a matter of perfecting it, of getting the kinks out. We'll reach the planets, and in our lifetimes too. How do you know what kind of crazy problems they run into two or three million miles from the Earth?"

Naturally, I had to admit I didn't know. All the newspapers had said was that both the First Martian and the two Venusian Expeditions had "experienced difficulties and been forced to return." I shut up and tried to think out another argument. That's all it was: the argument for me, and a business proposition for Fatty Myers. If you remember, back in March, the newspapers and magazines were still full of feature articles on "the expanding empire of man."

We reached the cove and Fatty locked his car. The sloop was all ready to go, as we'd fixed her up the night before. When we shoved off, she handled like a dream that Lipton might have had as a boy. She was gaff-rigged, but not too broad of beam so that we couldn't run a little if we wanted to. Fatty handled the tiller and I crewed. That way, we only needed ballast forward.

Neither of us were crazy about fishing. We'd made that up as an excuse for Edna. Sailing in the moonlight in the great, big loneliness of Cassowary Cove, with the smells of the Atlantic resting quietly around us—that was all the wallop we wanted.

"But suppose," I said, as soon as I'd trimmed sail, "suppose we got to Venus and there's a kind of animal there that finds us more appetizing than chili con carne. And suppose they're smarter than we are and have disintegrators and heat-rays like that fellow described in the story. And the minute they see us, they'll yell, 'Oh, boy—rations!' and come piling down on Earth.

"That'll do your business a lot of good, won't it? Why, when we get through driving them back off the planet, won't be a man or woman who'll be able to think of interplanetary travel without spitting. I go along with Reverend Pophurst: we shouldn't poke our noses into strange places where they were never meant to go or we'll get them bitten off."

Fatty thought a while and patted his stomach with his free hand like he always does when I score a good point. Most folks in town don't know it, but Fatty and I usually get so lathered up in arguments just before Election Day, that we always vote opposite tickets, no matter what.

"First place, if we hit animals smart enough to have disintegrators and such-like when we don't have them, *and* if they want this planet, they're going to take it away from us, and no movie hero in a tight jumper and riding boots is going to stop them at the last minute by discovering that the taste of pickled beets kills 'em dead. If they're smarter than we are and have more stuff, we'll be licked, that's all. We just won't be around any more, like the dinosaur. Second place, didn't you read Professor Fronac's article in last week's *Sunday Supplement?* He says there can't be any smarter animals— Say! What'd you call that? There, over to starboard?"

I turned and looked off to the right.

Where a streak of moonlight grinned on the water between the lips of the cove, something green and bulbous was coming in fast. It looked like the open top of an awfully big umbrella. I judged it to be thirty-five, forty feet across. It was floating straight for Mike's Casino on the southern lip where lights were blazing, music was banging, and people generally were having themselves a whale of a time.

"Seaweed," I guessed. "Bunch of seaweed all scrunched up in an ice-jam. Jam melted or broke up and it comes floating down here in one lump."

"Never saw that much seaweed in these parts." Fatty squinted at it. "Nor in that shape. And that bunch *came* into this cove; it didn't float in. The ocean's too quiet for it to have so much speed. Know what I think it is?"

"The first summer tourist?"

"No! A Portuguese man-of-war. They're jellyfish. They have a bladder, kind of, that floats on the surface, and long filaments underneath that trail into the water and catch fish. I've read about them but never expected to see one. Pretty rare around here. And that's a real big fellow. Want to take a look?"

"Not on your life! It may be dangerous. Besides, this is the first time in a month Edna's let me go out with you. She doesn't know exactly what's going to happen, but she's sure *something* is. I want to be home safe and sound by eleven. What were you saying about smarter animals, Fatty? On other planets?"

"It can't be dangerous," he muttered, still keeping his eyes on its track. "Only catches very small fish. But— Like I was saying, if there was something on Neptune, say which is more advanced than we are, why then it'd be smart enough to have space travel and they'd be visiting us instead of us them. Look how we've explored that planet. We've gone down into the ground nine miles and more, across every sea and into every ocean, back and forth over every piece of land, and now up into the air. If there was another kind of intelligent life on this Earth, we'd know it by now. Aliens with space travel would do the same. So, like Professor Fronac says, we must conclude— Am I wrong, or is that man-of-war coming at us now?"

It was. The green mass had turned in a great, rippling circle and was headed for our sloop, but fast.

Fatty slammed the tiller hard to starboard and I leaped for the sails. They went slack.

"What a time for the wind to drop!" he moaned. "There's a pair of emergency oars in the— Too late, it's abreast! You'll find a hatchet in the cockpit. See if you can—"

"I thought you said it wasn't dangerous," I puffed, as I scrambled back with the hatchet.

Fatty had dropped the tiller and picked up a marlinspike. He stood up next to me and stared at the floating mound alongside. Both it and our boat seemed to be perfectly still. We could see water rushing past us. Far off, in Mike's Casino, the band was playing "Did Your Mother Come From Ireland?" I stopped being sad and got sentimental. That song always makes me sentimental.

"It isn't dangerous," Fatty admitted. "But I just remembered that the Portùguese man-of-war has batteries of stingers that it uses to catch fish. They can hurt a man sometimes, too. And in anything this big— Of course, we're inside a boat and it can't get at us."

"You hope. Something tells me that I won't be home at eleven tonight. And if that's just supposed to be an air-filled bladder, what are those black things floating in it? Eyes?"

"They sure look like eyes. *Feel* like eyes." We watched the black dots flickering over the green surface and began to shuffle our feet. We felt as if a crowd of people were watching us undress in Courthouse Square. I know we both did, because we compared notes later. We had plenty of time—later.

"Know what?" Fatty said. "I don't think it's a Portuguese man-of-war, after all. It's too big and green, and I don't remember seeing anything like those black dots inside the air bladder in any of those pictures I saw. And it doesn't seem to have any filaments hanging from it. Besides, it moves too fast."

"Then what is it?"

Fatty patted his stomach and looked at it. He opened his mouth.

I forgot to ask him what he was going to say just then, and he never told me. He didn't say it anyway. He just went "Beep?" and sat down hard. I also sat down hard, only I went more like "Foof?"

The sloop had gone straight up in the air for about fifteen feet. As soon as I could, I jumped up and helped Fatty wheeze to a standing position.

We both gulped. The gulps seemed to get stuck going down.

Even though we were fifteen feet above the surface of the cove, the boat was still in the water. A little cup of water, that is, extending twenty feet out on both port and starboard and only about five feet on the bow and stern.

Beyond the water, there was a kind of gray haze that

was transparent enough for me to see the lights of Mike's Casino where they were still playing "Did Your Mother Come From Ireland?" This gray haze went all the way around, covering the mast and the gaff tops.

When we rushed over to the side and looked down, we saw it came around under the keel too. Solid stuff, that gray haze—it contained us, the boat and enough water to float it.

Somebody had taken an awfully big bite out of Cassowary Cove, and we were included. We knew who that somebody was. We looked around for him.

The big slob was busy outside the gray haze. First, he was under the keel, fastening a little box to the bottom of the haze. Then he squirmed around to the top, directly over the mast and stuck another doohickey up there. Those little black dots were still bubbling around inside his green body, but they didn't make me feel queer any more.

I had other things to feel queer about. "Do you think we might try yelling at him?" Fatty asked in the kind of whisper he uses in church. "Whatever he is, he looks intelligent."

"What could you yell?"

He scratched his head. "I dunno. How about, 'Friend. Me friend. No hurt. Peace.' Think he'd understand?"

"He'd think you were an Indian in the movies, that's what. Why should you think he understands English? Let's drop our weapons and raise both our hands. That gesture's universal, I read."

We kept our hands over our heads until they got tired. The lump of green jelly had moved from the box he had fixed over the mast to a position in line with the slant of the gaff. He boiled around for a few seconds until a section of the gray haze began to sparkle with color; a lot of colors, shifting in and out of each other. Then, as soon as the patch was coruscating nicely, he dropped off the side and hit the water fifteen feet below.

He hit the water without a splash.

He zoomed along the surface, faster than I could breathe the initials J. R., for about half a mile, paused just outside the cove—and dropped out of sight. There wasn't a ripple to show the path he'd been traveling, or where he'd sunk. All that was left was our floating gray bubble. With us, inside.

"Hey!" Fatty began yammering. "You can't do this to me! Come back and let us out, d'ye hear? Hey, you in that green jelly, come back here!"

I got him quiet by pointing out that the animated shrimp cocktail was no longer with us. Also, there didn't seem much cause for worry. If he'd wanted to do us any harm, he could pretty much have done it while he was close up, considering the brand of parlor tricks he had already demonstrated. Let well enough alone, I argued; I was satisfied to be alive and unwell, while the bubble-blowing object did a Weismuller somewhere in the Atlantic.

"But we can't stay here all night," Fatty complained. "Suppose someone from town could see us—why, with our reputation, they'd laugh us clear into the comic strips. Whyn't you shinny up the mast and stick an arm into that stuff, Paul? Find out what it's made of, maybe make a hole and wriggle through?"

That sounded reasonable. We sure had to do something. He bent down and gave me a boost. I wrapped my legs around the mast, grabbed handfuls of sail and dragged myself to the top. The mast ended just under the box outside of the gray haze.

"There's a purring noise coming from the box," I called down to Fatty. "Nothing inside it but silver wheels going round and round like the one in an electric meter. Only they're not attached to anything. They're floating at all kinds of angles to each other and spinning at different speeds."

I heard Fatty curse uncertainly, and I punched up into the grayness. I hurt my fist. I pulled my arm back, massaged it as my feet slipped and scrambled on the mast and sail, and stabbed up with a forefinger. I hurt my forefinger.

"Gray stuff hard?" Fatty asked.

Unprintably unprintable it was hard. I told him.

"Come on down and get the hatchet. You might be able to chop a hole."

"I don't think so. This fog is almost transparent and I don't think it's made of any material we know. Fact is, I don't think it's made of any material."

Above my head, the purring got a little louder. There was a similar noise coming from the bottom of the bubble where the other box was located.

I took a chance and, holding myself by one arm and one leg, I swung out and peered at the spot of shifting color near the box. It looked like the spectrum you see in an oil puddle—you know, colors changing their position while you look at them. I pushed up against the gray near the colored patch. It didn't give either.

The nasty thing was I had the feeling that it wasn't like trying to push a hole through a sheet of steel; it was more as if I were trying to drive a nail into an argument, or break a sermon across my knee. Kind of a joke in a scary sort of way.

"Hand up the hatchet," I called. "I don't see how it'll do any good, but I'll try it anyway."

Fatty lifted the hatchet high and stood up on his toes. I started to slide down the mast. The purring from the box became a whine.

Just as my stretching fingers closed around the hatchet handle, the box on top and the box on the bottom of the boat began going *clinkety-clangety-clung*. It reached *clung*

and I was no longer doing it to the mast. I was on top of
Fatty and he was spread-eagled on the deck.

I had a glimpse of the hatchet sailing over the side.

"Wh-what f-for you wanted to d-do th-that," Fatty
gasped as I rolled off him and we both groaned upright.
"C-couldn't you tell me you w-wanted to get down fast?
I'd have moved away, honest!"

"Wasn't my fault," I said. "I was pushed."

Fatty wasn't listening. He was staring at something else.
And, when I noticed it, so was I.

A lot of sea-water had splashed into the cockpit. Some
of it had wet us.

All of the water on deck rolled into a little lake abaft of
the mast, the water on our bodies dripping down and
joining it. Then, the entire puddle rolled to port and
spilled off the deck. The boat was perfectly dry again. So
were we.

"This I'm beginning not to like," Fatty commented
hoarsely. I nodded my head, too. Under the circumstances
I didn't feel easy in my mind.

Stepping very delicately, as if he were afraid he might
fracture a commandment, Fatty moved over to the side
and looked out. He shook his head and looked down.

"Paul," he said after a while in a low voice. "Paul,
would you come here? Something I—" he choked.

I took a look. I gulped, one of those really long gulps
that start down from your Adam's apple and wind up
squishing out between your toes.

Below us, under the water and the gray haze, was a
slew of darkness. Beyond that, at a respectable distance, I
could see the Atlantic Ocean and the New England coast-
line with Cape Cod hooking out its small, bent finger.
New England was moving away fast and became the
eastern seaboard of the United States even as I watched.

The moonlight gave it a sort of unhealthy dimness, just
enough to make out details and recognize the North and

South American continents when they grew out of the eastern seaboard. The western coast was a little dark and blurry, but it made me homesick for the days when Fatty and Edna and I sat next to a map looking just like that in school.

Right then, I couldn't think of anything more absolutely enjoyable than standing near Edna in the grocery while she nagged the ears off me.

"That's what happened," Fatty was whimpering. "That's why we fell and the water jumped into the boat. We just shot up in a straight line suddenly and we're still traveling—us, the sloop, and enough water to float the whole business. We're inside a gray ball that isn't made of anything and which we can't break out of even if we still wanted to."

"Take it easy, Fatty, and we'll be all right," I told him with all the assurance of a bank robber trying to explain to the policeman who caught him that he was only trying to deposit his gun in the vault and the cashiers misunderstood him.

We sat down heavily in the cockpit and Fatty automatically grabbed the tiller. He sighed and shook his head.

"I feel just like a package being sent some place." He gestured up towards the spot of changing color. "And that's the label. Please do not open until Christmas."

"What is it, do you think? An invasion from another planet?"

"And we're the first battle? Don't be silly, Paul. Altough a nut Earth might be. The careless, offhand way sent back to headquarters to give them an idea of how tough a nut Earth might be. The careless, offhand way that green whatnot acted is what gripes me! It was as if he was going after Mike's Casino first and then decided to take us because we were closer, or because our disappearance would attract less notice than a night-club's. But either way it didn't matter much. He did it and went back home, or—"

"I can still hear Mike's Casino. At least I can hear the band playing 'Did Your Mother Come From Ireland?' "

Fatty slanted his big, loose face at the mast. "I hear it too. But it's coming from that box with the wheels up there. This whole thing is so crazy, Paul: I'm beginning to think that creature knew it was your favorite song and fixed the box to play it all the time. So you'd be more comfortable, kind of. Like the glow we have inside the bubble to provide us with light. He wants the package to arrive in good condition."

"A space-going juke-box," I muttered.

There was a longish bit of silence after that. We sat and watched the stars go by. I tried to make out the Big Dipper but it must have been lost in the shuffle, or maybe its position was different up here. The Moon was shrinking off to port, so I decided we weren't going there. Not that it made much difference. But at least there was an Army base on the Moon and I've seen enough western films to have great confidence in the United States Army—at least in the cavalry part. The sun wasn't a pleasant sight from empty space.

The funny thing is that neither of us were really frightened. It was partly the suddenness with which we'd been wrapped up and mailed, partly the care that was being taken of us. Inside the bubble there was a glow like broad daylight, strong enough to read by.

Fatty sat and worried about the option on the Winthrop store he'd lose if he didn't pick it up in time. I figured out explanations for Edna on why I didn't make it home by eleven. The box on top and the box on bottom hummed and mumbled. The sloop maintained the position it had originally had in Cassowary Cove, perfectly steady in the water. Every once in a while, Fatty bit a fingernail and I tied a shoelace.

No, we weren't really frightened—there didn't seem to be anything solid enough to get frightened about, sitting in a sailboat out there with trillions of tiny lights burning all around. But we sure would have given our right arms clear up to our left hands for a sneak preview of the next act.

"One consolation, if you can call it that," Fatty said. "There's some sort of barrier two or three million miles from the Earth and this contraption may not be able to get past it. The papers don't say exactly what the spaceships hit out here, but I gathered it was something that stopped them cold, but didn't smash them and allowed them to turn and come back. Something like—like—"

"Like the stuff this gray bubble is made of," I suggested. We stared at each other for a few minutes, then Fatty found an unbitten nail on one of his fingers and took care of it, and I tied both my shoelaces.

We got hungry. There was nothing in our pockets that could be eaten. That made us hungrier.

Fatty lumbered over to the side and looked down into the water. "Just as I thought. Hey, Paul, break out your fishing tackle. There's a mackerel swimming around under the boat. Must have been caught up with us."

"Fishing'll take too long. I'll net it." I undressed, grabbed my landing net. "There's not much water and he won't have maneuvering space. But what about a fire? If we try to cook it, won't we use up the air?"

He shook his head. "Nope. We've been in long enough for the air to foul if it wasn't being changed. It's as fresh as ever. Whatever that machinery is up there, it's not only tooling us along at a smart clip and playing 'Did Your Mother Come From Ireland?' for your special benefit, but it's also pumping fresh air in and stale air out. And if you ask me where it gets oxygen and nitrogen in empty space—"

"I wouldn't dream of it," I assured him.

As soon as I spied the mackerel, a small one, less than a foot long, I stepped into the water and went for it with the net. I'm a pretty good underwater swimmer.

Pretty good, but the mackerel was better. More practice. I felt silly caroming off the keel and gray haze while the fish dodged all around me. After a while, he got positively insulting. He actually swam backward, facing me, just out of reach of the net.

I came to the surface, swallowed air, and climbed back aboard.

"He's too spry," I began. "I'll get my fishing gear and—"

I stopped. I was back in the gulping groove again.

Fatty was sitting in the cockpit, looking as if he had sat down suddenly. In front of him there was a flock of plates, six glasses and two snowy napkins on which rested assorted knives, forks and spoons.

There were two glasses of water, two glasses of milk and two glasses of beer. The plates were filled with food: grapefruit, soup, beef steak, French fried potatoes, green peas, and—for dessert—ice cream. Enough for two. Our dream meal.

"It came from the box above," Fatty told me as I dressed with clumsy fingers. "I heard a click and looked up. There was this stuff floating down in single file. They distributed themselves evenly as they hit the deck."

"At least they feed you well."

Fatty grimaced at me. "You know where else you get served a meal with everything your heart desires."

Well, we unwrapped the cutlery and ate. What else could we do? The food was delicious, perfectly cooked. The drinks and the ice cream were cold, the grapefruit was chilled. When we finished, there was another click. First, three cigars that I remembered smoking at Louisa Capek's birthday party and liking more than any others

I'd ever had, then, a plug of Fatty Myers's favorite chaw appeared. When the matches breezed down, we had stopped shrugging our shoulders. Fatty talked to himself a little, though.

I was halfway through the first cigar when Fatty heaved himself upright. "Got an idea."

He picked up a couple of plates and heaved them over the side. We both stood and watched them sink. Just before they got to the bottom—they disappeared. Like that. About two feet away from the lower box.

"So that's what happens to the waste."

"What?" I asked him.

He glared at me. "That."

We got rid of the rest of the service in the same way. On Fatty's suggestion we kept the knives. "We might need weapons when we arrive where—where we're going. Characters there might want to dissect us, or torture information out of us about Earth."

"If they can pull this kind of stuff, do you think we can stop them?" I wanted to know. "With knives that they made up for us out of empty emptiness?"

But we kept the knives.

We also kept the mackerel. For a pet. If we were going to be fed this as a steady diet, who wanted mackerel? There were only the three of us in that bubble and we felt we all had to stick together. The mackerel felt it too, for he began swimming up near the surface whenever we came close to the side. We became pretty good friends, and I fed him the bait I'd brought along—free.

About four hours later—it may have been five, because neither Fatty nor I had watches—the box clicked and the same meal wafted down with all the fixings. We ate some and threw the rest overboard.

"You know," Fatty said. "If it weren't for that 'Did Your Mother Come From Ireland' playing over and over, I could almost be enjoying myself."

"Yeah. I'm getting tired of it myself. But would you rather be listening to 'I'm Forever Blowing Bubbles'?"

The Earth was just a shrinking, shining disc but neither of us could resist grabbing a fast look at it, now and then. It meant my grocery and Edna, Fatty's service station and his option on the Winthrop store. Home, 'mid planets and galaxies. . . .

We got sleepy and pulled down the sails which weren't being overwhelmingly useful at the time. We rolled them up into a sort of mattress and, together with some blankets Fatty had in the cockpit, made ourselves a fairish bed.

When we woke out of a mutual nightmare in which Fatty and I were being dissected by a couple of oyster stews, there were two complete steak dinners on deck. That is, two for me and two for Fatty. We had a grapefruit and a glass of milk apiece and got rid of the rest. We lounged around uncomfortably and cursed the composer of 'Did Your Mother Come From Ireland?' I couldn't understand how I'd ever liked that song.

I didn't think too much of the sloop, either. It was one of the most idiotic boats I'd ever seen, narrow, hard, uninteresting lines. If I ever bought a boat it wouldn't be a sloop.

We shucked our clothes off and went for a swim around the edges. Fatty floated on his back, his immense belly rising above the surface, while I dived down and played tag with the mackerel.

Around us was nothing but the universe. Stars, stars and still more stars. I'd have given anything for a street light.

We climbed back in the boat to find another steak dinner waiting. The swim had made us hungry, so we ate about a quarter of it.

"Not very efficient," Fatty grumbled. "I mean that green monster. Some way or other—telepathy, maybe—he figured we liked certain things. Steak dinners, special tobacco, a song. He didn't bother to go into it any further and find out how *much* of those things we liked—and how often. Careless workmanship."

"Talk about carelessness," I shot at him. "You wanted to go out and take a look at him when he first came into the cove. You were at the tiller and couldn't even get us about in time. You didn't see he was chasing us until he was abreast!"

His little eyes boiled red. "I was at the tiller, but what were you doing right then? You were pretty unoccupied and you should have seen him coming! But did you?"

"Hah! You thought he was a Portuguese man-of-war. Like the time we were shingling the church roof and you thought that the black spot near the steeple was a sheet of metal when all the time it was only a hole. We wouldn't have fallen past the beam either, if you weren't such a big fat slob."

Fatty stood up and waved his stomach at me. "For a little hen-pecked squirt, you sure— Hey, Paul, don't let's get going this way. We don't know how long we may have to be together on this flea-bitten rowboat and we don't want to start arguing."

He was right. I apologized. "My fault, that church roof—"

"No, *my* fault," he insisted generously. "I *was* a little too heavy at that moment. Shake, old pal, and let's keep our heads. We'll be the only representatives of humanity wherever we're heading, and we have to stick together."

We shook and had a glass of beer on it.

All the same, it did get tight as steak dinner followed steak dinner and 'Did Your Mother Come From Ireland?' went through chorus after chorus. We carved a checkerboard out of some deck boards and tore up old newspapers to make checkers. We went for swims around the boat, and we made up little guessing games to try on each other. We tested the gray haze and thought up a thousand different ways that the boxes might be working, a thousand different explanations of the spot of color near the top, a thousand different reasons for our being bubbled and sent out into the wild black yonder.

But we were down to counting stars when the red planet began to grow large.

"Mars," Fatty said. "It looks like the picture of Mars in the article Professor Fronac had in the *Sunday Supplement*."

"I wish he was here instead of us. He wanted to go to Mars. We didn't."

There wasn't a cloud in the sky on Mars as we came down through the clearest air I've ever seen. We landed ever so gently in a flat desert of red sand. On all sides of the gray ball we could see acres on acres of sand.

Nothing else.

"Don't know if this is much of an improvement on what we've been through," I remarked morosely.

Fatty wasn't listening. He was standing on his toes and staring around eagerly.

"We're seeing what no man has ever seen before us," he said softly. "We're on Mars, do you understand, Paul? The sun—notice how much smaller it looks than on Earth? What wouldn't Professor Fronac give to be in our shoes!"

"He can have mine any time he shows up. And I'll throw in a new pair of soles and heels. Looking at a red desert isn't my idea of a really big time, if you know what I mean. Gives me no bang at all. And where are the Martians?"

"They'll show, Paul, they'll show. They didn't send us forty million miles just to decorate their desert. Hold your horses, feller."

But I didn't have to hold them long. Off at the edge of the horizon, two specks appeared, one in the air and coming fast, and one mooching along the ground.

The speck in the air grew into a green and bulbous mass about the size of the one in Cassowary Cove. It didn't have any wings or jets or any other way of pushing itself along that I could see. It just happened to be flying.

When it reached us, the one on the ground was still far away.

Our new buddy had eyes, too—if that's what they were. Only they weren't black dots floating inside it; they were dark knob-like affairs stuck on the outside. But they felt just the same as the other when it paused on top of our bubble—as if they could undress our minds.

Just a second of this. Then it moved to the box, fiddled with it a moment and the music stopped. The silence sounded wonderful.

When it slid round to the bottom, going down through the sand as if the desert was made of mirage, Fatty handed me a couple of the knives we'd saved and picked out three for himself.

"Stand by," he whispered. "It may come off any minute now."

I didn't make any sarcastic crack about the usefulness of such weapons because I was having trouble breathing. Besides, the knives gave me a little confidence. I couldn't see where we might go if we happened to have a battle with these things and won, but it was nice holding some-thing that could conceivably do damage.

By this time, the guy on the ground had arrived. He was in a one-wheeled car that was filled with wires and gadgets and crackly stuff. We didn't get a good glimpse of him until he stepped out of the car and stood stiffly against it.

When we did, we didn't like it. This whole play was getting peculiar.

He wasn't green and he wasn't bulbous. He was about half our height, very thin, shaped like a flexible cylinder. He was blue, streaked with white, and about a dozen tentacles trailed out from the middle of the cylinder under a battery of holes and bumps that I figured were the opposite number of ears, noses and mouths.

He stood on a pedestal of small cylinder that seemed to have a sucking bottom to grip the sand.

When our green friend had finished working on the underside, he came tearing up to Jo-Jo near the car. Jo-Jo stiffened even more for a second, then seemed to get all loose and flexible and bent over, his tentacles drooping on the sand.

It wasn't a bow. It reminded me more of the way a dog fawns.

"They *could* have two intelligent races here on Mars," Fatty suggested in a low voice.

Then, while the tentacled chap was still scraping desert, the blob of green lifted and skimmed away in the direction he'd come. It was exactly like the business back in Cassowary Cove, except this time it was flying away while back on Earth it had zoomed along the water and submerged. But both were done so quickly and carelessly as to be positively insulting. After all, I'm not exactly small potatoes in my part of the country: one of my ancestors would have come over on the *Mayflower* if he hadn't been in jail.

This cylinder character turned and watched until the jellyfish was out of sight. Very slowly, he turned back again and looked at us. We shuffled our feet.

Our visitor began piling equipment out of the car and on the sand. He fitted this in that, one doojigger into another doohickey. A crazy-angled, shiny machine took shape which was moved against our little gray home away from home. He climbed into it and twirled thingumajigs with his tentacles.

A small bubble formed around the machine, attached to the gray haze.

"Air-lock," Fatty told me. "He's making an air-lock so that he can come in without having our air belch into the desert. Mars has no atmosphere to speak of."

He was right. An opening appeared in the grayness and Kid Tentacles sucked through slightly above water level. He was suspended in the air like that for a while, considering us.

Without warning, he dropped down into the water—only he splashed—and out of sight. We hurried to the side and looked down.

He was resting on the bottom, all his tentacles extended out at the mackerel which was scrunched up hard against the wall of gray, its tail curved behind it. A bunch of bubbles dripped up to the surface from the cylinder's mid-section and burst.

I didn't get it. "Wonder what he wants of that poor mackerel. He's sure scaring it silly. It must think he's the Grim Angler."

The moment I'd opened my mouth, the blue and white fellow started rising. He came up over the side and hit our deck with a wet sound from the base of his pedestal.

A couple of tentacles uncoiled at us. We moved back. One of the holes in his midsection expanded, twisted like a mouth in the middle of a stutter. Then in a rumbling, terrifically deep bass:

"You—ah—are the intelligent life from Earth? Ah, I did not expect two."

"English!" we both yelped.

"Correct language? Ah, I think so. You—ah, are New English, but English is correct language. This language has been dreefed into me—ah, dreefed is not right—so that I could adjust correctly. But excuse me. Ah, I only expected one and I didn't know whether you were marine or land form. Ah, I though at first— Permit me: my name is Blizel-Ri-Ri-Bel."

"Mine's Myers," Fatty stepped forward and shook a tentacle, taking control of the situation as he always did. "This is my pal, Paul Garland. I guess you're here to give us the score?"

"To give you the score," Blizel echoed. "To adjust. To make the choice. To explain. To—"

Fatty raised a pudgy hand and headed him off. "What happened to the other Martian?"

Blizel coiled two of his tentacles into a braid. "No, ah, other Martian, that. I am Martian, ah, and representative of Martian Government. It-Of-Shoin is Ambassador from Shoin."

"Shoin?"

"Shoin. Galactic nation, ah, of which our system is a province. Shoin is nation of this galaxy and other galaxies. Ah, it in turn is part of larger nation whose name we do not know. It-Of-Shoin, the, ah, ambassador, has, ah, already decided which of you will be best but has not told me. Ah, I must make choice myself to prove partially our capabilities, ah, and our readiness to assume complete citizenship in Shoin. This is difficult as we, ah, are but five times as advanced as you, to round the numbers."

"You want to find out which of us is best? For what?"

"To stay as diplomatic functionary so that your people will be able to come here and there as they could now, but for the barrier of forces in balance which has been dreefed, ah, about your planet and satellite. This barrier has protected you from unwarranted intrusion, ah, as well as prevented you from unexpectedly, ah, appearing in a civilized part of Shoin to your detriment. It-Of-Shoin on your planet has been more interested in observing the development of the intelligent life forms at the core of your planet than on its surface, no discredit, ah, intended. It-Of-Shoin was unaware you had acquired space travel."

"It-Of-Shoin on Earth," Fatty mused. "The one who sent us here. The Ambassador to Earth, hey?"

The Martian twisted his tentacles in genuine embarrassment. His white streaks got broader. "Ah, Earth does not require an ambassador as yet. It-Of-Shoin is, ah, a—yes, a consul. To all the intelligent life forms of, ah, Earth. Ah, I will return."

He plopped backward into the smaller bubble which was his air lock and started collecting machinery.

Fatty and I compared notes.

All of our galaxy and several others were part of a federation called "Shoin." Mars was practically ready to join or be accepted into the federation whose other members they considered pretty terrific operators. Earth was a backward planet and only rated a consul who was an "It-From-Shoin." He had a much higher regard for several other specimens of life he'd found on our planet than for man. Nevertheless, we'd surprised him by giving out with space ships long before we should have. These ships hadn't been able to go anywhere else than the Moon because of something called "forces-in-balance" which acted as a barrier both within and without.

For some reason, a representative of Earth was needed on Mars. This consul had scooted up one night and grabbed us off. When we'd arrived on Mars, the Shoinian ambassador had inspected us and decided which he wanted. Did that mean that one of us could return? And what about the other?

Anyway, he was too all-fired superior to tell the Martians which was the lucky man. He'd taught some government official our language by "dreefing" and it was up to the Martian from then on. The Martian, for all his humbleness, thought he was at least five times as good as we were. Finally, his English wasn't too good.

"Maybe he was only dreefed once," I suggested. "And it didn't take." I was nervous: we were still being treated too casually.

"What's with this dreefing?" Fatty asked Blizel when he plopped back on deck with a couple of tentacleloads of equipment.

"They-Of-Shoin alone can dreef. We, ah, of Mars must use machinery still. Dreef is not the image but a construction of an, ah, of a transliteration for your delight. They-Of-Shoin dreef by, ah, utilizing force-patterns of what you call cosmos? Thus any product can be realized into, ah, existence—whether material or otherwise. Now testing for you."

The Martian was presenting us with various gadgets on which colored lights flickered. We found that he wanted us to match switches with the colored lights in certain patterns but we couldn't seem to get any of them right.

While he was playing around with the toys, Fatty asked innocently what would happen if we refused to split up and leave one of us here. The Martian replied innocently: one of us *would* be left here, as we had no choice since we couldn't do a thing unless we were allowed to by them.

Fatty told him of the presence on Earth of very brilliant men who knew calculus and suchlike and would give both eyeteeth and maybe an eye or so for the chance to spend their lives on Mars. These men, he pointed out, would be much more interesting for the Martians to have around, maybe even for They-Of-Shoin too, than a small-town grocer and gas-station owner who had both flunked elementary algebra.

"Ah, I think," Blizel delicately commented, "that you overestimate the gulf between their intellects and yours, in our views."

Fatty was elected. His experience with motors turned the trick. I congratulated him. He looked miserably at me.

Blizel withdrew, saying that he expected Fatty to go with him on a little trip to their "slimp"—which we decided was a city of sorts. He would bring Fatty back to "ah, organize farewell" if it turned out that Fatty was the right candidate. He was awfully nervous about the whole proposition himself.

Fatty shook his round head at the Martian who was building a small bubble outside of ours for transportation purposes.

"You know, we can't really blame those guys. They have troubles of their own, after all. They're trying to get into a galactic federation on equal terms with some big shots and they want to prove themselves. They feel like rookies going into a game with a world-series pitcher to bat against. But I don't get the way they crawl and suck around these Shoiners. They need a little backbone. When you come right down to it, they're nothing but exploited natives, and everyone thinks we'll be the same, but on a lower level."

"Wait'll we get here. We'll stiffen these Martians, Fatty. We'll get the system free of galactic imperialists, with our atom bombs and all. Bet our scientists have this forces-in-balance thing licked in no time. And dreefing, too."

"Sure. Think of it—another life-form, maybe more than one, in the core of the Earth with this It-From-Shoin leading them around by the noses or whatever. Golly! And these Martians here with their civilization, and no telling what other intelligent characters we have scattered between Mercury and Pluto. A whole empire, Paul, bigger than anything on Earth—all controlled by those green jellies!"

Blizel finished building the bubble and Fatty went into it through the air-lock. It was darker than the one he left behind. I guessed Blizel wasn't as skilled as that fellow down in Cassowary Cove.

The Martian got back into his machine and started off. Fatty's bubble floated along above it.

I spent about ten or twelve hours on Mars alone. Night fell, and I watched two moons chase across the sky. Some sort of big snake wriggled up out of the sand, looked at me and went away on his own private big deal.

No more steak dinners came down, and I actually found myself missing the stuff.

When Fatty and Blizel returned, the Martian stayed outside and tinkered with the equipment. Fatty came back through the air-lock slowly.

He was licking his lips and sighing in half-breaths. I got scared.

"Fatty, did they harm you? Did they do anything drastic?"

"No, Paul, they didn't," he said quietly. "I've just been through a—well, a *big* experience."

He patted the mast gently before continuing. "I've seen the slimp, and it's really not a city, not as we understood cities. It's as much like New York or Boston as New York or Boston is like an ant-hill or bee-hive. Just because Blizel spoke our language so very damn poorly, we had him pegged as a sort of ignorant foreigner. Paul, it's not that way at all. These Martians are so far above us, beyond us, that I'm amazed. They've had space travel for thousands of years. They've been to the stars and every planet in the system that isn't restricted. Uranus and Earth are restricted. Barriers.

"But they have colonies and scientists on all the others. They have atomic power and stuff after atomic power and stuff after that. And yet they look up to these fellows from Shoin so much that you can just begin to imagine. They're not exploited, just watched and helped. And these fellows from Shoin, they're part of a bigger federation which I don't quite understand, and they're watched and guarded and helped too—by other things. The universe is old, Paul, and we're newcomers, such terribly new newcomers!

Think of what it will do to our pride when we find it out."

There was a dollop of quietness while Fatty slapped the mast and I frowned at him. They must have done something to the poor guy, his backbone had just slipped right out. Some devilish machine, they probably had. Once Fatty was back on Earth he'd be normal again—the same old cocky Fatty Myers.

"Are—are you acceptable?"

"Yeah, I'm acceptable. The ambassador—It-From-Shoin," he said with more respect in his voice than I'd ever heard before, "says I'm the one he picked. You should have seen the way Blizel and his crowd bucked up when they heard that! Now you have to get back to Earth. Blizel will fix the bubble so you'll have more variety in your meals and can let them know what's what. When humans start coming here regularly, they can appoint another man to handle affairs and, if he's acceptable to Shoin and Mars, I can go back."

"Fatty, what if I can't get anyone to believe me?"

He shrugged. "I don't know what happens in that case. Blizel tells me that if you can't operate successfully enough to get man through the barrier in a riz or two, they will conclude that he isn't enough of an intellect as yet to warrant their interest. You've just got to do it, Paul, because I don't know what happens to me if you don't, and from what I can see, nobody up here cares much."

"Meanwhile, you'll be all right?"

"I'll be preparing a sort of city for Earthmen to live in on Mars. If you send any folks in the right channels, I'm supposed to verify them and greet them when they arrive. I'll explain the setup as one human to another. Makes me out as an official greeter, doesn't it?"

After Blizel finished tinkering with the boxes, he applied another spot of color near the top and I shot away from Mars. The return trip was pretty boring, and the mackerel died on the way. There were a lot of different dishes served, and I was able to keep up my interest in food, but everything had a soapy taste.

Blizel just wasn't up to that guy in Cassowary Cove, no two ways about it.

I landed on the same spot from which we'd taken off—two months before, as I found.

The bubble dissolved as I hit the water. I didn't bother to sail the sloop in, but dived off the deck and swam ashore.

It felt good to be able to swim a distance in a straight line.

It seems that there were folks who wanted to hold a funeral for us, but Edna had put her foot down. She insisted that so long as no wreckage was found, she'd consider me alive.

I'd probably turn up in Europe one fine day with Fatty, she told them.

So when I walked into the grocery, being Edna, she merely turned to face me. She asked me where I'd been. Mars, I said. She hasn't spoken to me since.

A reporter from our local paper interviewed me that night and wrote up a crazy story about how I'd claimed I had established consulates all over the solar system. I hadn't; I'd just told him my friend Fatty Myers was the acting-consul for Earth on Mars.

The story was reprinted in one of the Boston papers as a little back-page squib with a humorous illustration. That's all. I've been going crazy since trying to get someone to believe me.

Remember, there's a time limit: one riz, two at the most.

For the last time, then, to anyone who's interested in space travel after all I've said: Stop knocking yourself out trying to break through a barrier of forces-in-balance that isn't meant to be broken through. You have to come down to Cassowary Cove and take a boat out and wait for It-From-Shoin to appear. I'll help, and you can be sure that when it gets to him, Fatty Myers will verify and do whatever else is necessary. But you won't be able to go to Venus or Mars any other way.

You need a visa.

THE LEMON-GREEN...

...in. Cover and tare it boat, anyway, anymore ... I'll stand off to see-place. I'll help, and see you see the site...
how even to ask to ask... Ruth Martisti writin... see... X...

THE
LEMON-GREEN
SPAGHETTI-LOUD
DYNAMITE-DRIBBLE
DAY

Testimony of Witness No. 5671 before the Special Presidential Investigative Commission. Leonard Drucker, thirty-one years old, unmarried, of 238 West 10th Street, New York City, Borough of Manhattan, employed as a salesman by the Har-Bern Office Partition Company of 205 East 42nd Street, New York City, Borough of Manhattan. Witness, being placed under oath, does swear and depose:

WELL, I don't know, the telephone woke me up about eight A.M. on that Wednesday morning. I grabbed at it, half falling out of bed, and finally managed to juggle it up to my ear. A girl's voice was saying, "Hello, Lennie? Is that you, Lennie? Hello?"

After a couple of seconds, I recognized the voice. I said, "Doris? Yeah, it's me. What's the matter?"

"You tell me, Lennie!" She sounded absolutely hysterical. "Have you been listening to the radio? I called up three people already and they're just as bad as the radio. You sure you're all right?"

"I'm fine. Hey, it's eight o'clock—I had another fifteen minutes sleep. And my coffee—it's in the percolator. Let me turn the—the—"

"You too!" she screeched. "It's affected you too! What's the matter with everybody? What's happening?" And she hung up.

I put down the phone and shuddered. Doris was a girl I'd been seeing, and she'd looked very normal. Now it was obvious she was just another kooky Village chick. I may live in the Village, but I hold down a good job and I dress conservatively. Usually, I stay far away from kooky Village chicks.

There was no point in going back to sleep, so I flipped

the switch gizmo on my electric percolator and turned it on. That, I guess, is the crucial part of this testimony. You see, I always set up my coffee percolator the night before and fill it with water. When I get up in the morning, I'm too blind and dopey to cook anything.

Because of Doris's call, I also flicked on the radio before I went into the bathroom. I splashed some cold water on my face, rinsed out my toothbrush, and put some toothpaste on it. It was halfway to my mouth when I began listening to the radio. I put it down on the sink and went out and sat next to the radio, really fascinated. I never brushed my teeth: I was one lucky son of a bitch all around.

The radio announcer had a warm, sleepy voice. He was enunciating carefully: ". . . forty-eight . . . forty-nine . . . *forty!* Forty-one . . . forty-two . . . forty-three . . . forty-four . . . forty-five . . . forty-six . . . forty-seven . . . forty-eight . . . forty-nine . . . *forty!* Forty-one . . ."

I stayed with that voice, I don't know, for a long time. It didn't ever get up to fifty. The coffee had finished perking, so I poured myself a cup and sat and twirled the dial. Some of the stations—they were the Jersey ones, I found out later—sounded pretty much as usual, but most of the broadcasts were wild. There was a traffic report, I remember, that just gripped me.

". . . and on the Major Deegan Expressway, traffic is moderate to spaghetti-loud. All dynamite-dribbles are reported moving smoothly. The Cadillacs are longer, the Continentals are thinner, and the Chrysler Imperials have mostly snapped in two. Five thousand Chevrolet convertibles are building a basketball court in one uptown lane of the Franklin D. Roosevelt Drive. . . ."

While I was having another cup of coffee and some cookies, I happened to glance at my watch, and I realized almost an hour had slipped by with that damn radio! I gave myself a one-two-three shave with the electric razor and started dressing frantically.

I thought of calling Doris back to tell her she was right, but I thought, better not, better get to work first. And you know something? I never saw or heard from Doris again. I wonder what happened to *her* on that day. Well, she wasn't the only one. Right?

There was hardly anyone on the street, just a few people sitting on the curb with funny expressions on their faces. But I passed that big garage between my apartment house and the subway station, and there I stopped dead. It's one of the most expensive car hangars in the Village and it looked like, I don't know, a junkyard soufflé.

In the dimness, I could see cars mashed against cars, cars mashed against walls. Broken glass mixed in with strips of torn-off chrome. Fenders ripped off, hoods sprung open and all twisty.

Charlie, the attendant, came dragging out of his cubicle and kind of grinned at me. He looked as if he'd tied one on last night.

"Wait'll your boss sees this," I told him. "Man, you'll be dead."

He pointed at two cars locked together nose to nose near the entrance. "Mr. Carbonaro was here. He kept asking them to go on making love. When they wouldn't, he said to hell with them, he was going home. He was crying just like a milk bottle."

It was turning into one weird morning. I was only half surprised when there was no one on duty in the subway change booth. But I had a token on me. I put it in the turnstile and clunked through.

And that's when I first began to get scared—on the platform of the subway station. Whatever else is going on in the world, to a New Yorker the subway is a kind of man-made natural phenomenon, routine and regular as the sun coming up. And when the routine and regularity stop in the subway you sure as hell notice it.

Like the guy on his hands and knees at one end of the platform staring up a woman's dress, she rocking on high heels and singing a song to the ceiling. Or this pretty young Negro girl, sitting on a wooden bench, crying her heart out and wiping her eyes with great big newsprinted sheets of that morning's *Times*. Or the doctor-lawyer type running a slalom in and out of the iron pillars of the platform. He was chanting, "Chug, chug, chug-azoom, chug, chug, chug-azoom." And nobody in the station being startled, or even looking worried.

Three trains in a row came in and went right on through without stopping, without even slowing down. The engineer of the last one was a big, white-haired guy who was laughing his head off as he flashed past. Then a fourth train came in, and this one stopped.

Only two of us on the platform made a dash for it: me and a young fellow in khaki pants and a brown sweater. The doors opened and shut, *zip-zip,* practically in the same motion. The train took off without us.

"What's going on?" the young fellow whined at me. "I'm late for work—I had to run out of the house without any breakfast. But I can't get a train. I paid my fare. Why can't I get a train?"

I told him I didn't know, and I left him and went upstairs. I was very scared. I got into a phone booth and tried to call my office. The phone rang for a long time: no answer.

Then I wandered around on that corner near the subway station for a while, trying to decide what I should do next, trying to figure out what was happening. I kept calling the office. No luck. That was damn funny—it was way after nine o'clock. Maybe no one at all had come in today? I couldn't imagine such a thing.

I began noticing that the people going by on the street

had a funny sort of stare, a kind of pop-eyed, trancy look. Charlie, the garage man, he'd had it. But the kid in the brown sweater on the subway platform, he didn't have it. I saw a mirror in a store window and looked at myself. I didn't have it.

The store was a television repair place. They had a television set in the window, tuned into a program, and I got all involved in watching it. I don't know what the program was—two men and a woman were standing around talking to each other, but the woman was doing a slow strip. She was talking and peeling off her clothes at the same time. She had trouble with the garter belt and the men helped her.

Next door, there was a liquor store. People were going in and out, buying a lot of liquor. But then I saw that buying wasn't exactly the right word. What they'd do, they'd walk in, shoot a quick, suspicious look at the owner, grab up a couple of bottles—and walk out. The owner was watching them do this with a big, beaming smile.

A guy came out with a couple of fifths, a stinking, dirty guy, strictly a Bowery type. He was all happy—you know, the millennium.

We both saw the other didn't have the pop-eyed look. (This was the first time, but all that day I had a lot of those flashes of recognition. You immediately noticed someone without the pop-eyed look.)

"It's great, hah?" he said. "All over town. Help yourself, fella, help yourself to the sauce. You know whatsamatter with em, hah?"

I stared at his maybe three, maybe five teeth. "No. What?"

"They've been drinking water. It's finally caught up with them. Poison, pure poison. I always said it. You know the last time I had a glass of water? You know, hah? Over twelve years ago."

I just turned my back and took off and left him standing there.

Walking fast, uptown on Sixth, I said to myself, where the hell am I going? I decided to go to my office on 42nd Street. It's like when there was a subway strike. I still belonged at the office.

For a while I looked out for a taxi, but you know, there were damn few cars going up the avenue, and most of them were traveling very, very slowly. Once in a while, there'd be one going fast, highway speed or beyond. Plenty of accidents.

The first accident I saw, I ran over to see if I could help. But the driver had already crawled out. He looked at the fire hydrant he'd knocked over, he looked at it spouting and shook himself and staggered away. After that I passed up the accidents. I just kept an eye out to see that no cars were coming up on the sidewalk after me.

But that geyser of water made me think of what the bum had said. Was it something in the water? I'd had coffee, but I'd set up the percolator the night before. And I hadn't had time to brush my teeth. Doris, the guy in the brown sweater in the subway, they hadn't eaten breakfast yet, they hadn't touched water. Neither had the bum. It had to be the water.

I didn't know anything then about that bunch of LSD kids, you know, one of them being the daughter of a Water Supply engineer and getting her hands on her father's charts and all the other stuff that's come out. That poor guy! But I knew about enough to stay away from anything that used water from a tap. So, just in case, I stopped in at a self-service grocery and got a six-pack of soda, you know, cans with pull-open tops.

The clerk was looking at the back wall in a trance. He had such a scared expression on his face it almost made my hair stand up. I waited for him to start screaming, but he didn't. I walked out and left a dollar on the counter.

A block further on, I stopped to watch a fire.

It was in one of those small, scabby loft buildings that line lower Sixth. There were no flames visible, just a continuous balloon of smoke coming out of a third-floor window. A crowd of sleepy, dopey-looking people were in front of the place, mixed in with a bunch of bored, dopey-looking firemen. The big red fire engine was all the way up on the sidewalk with its nose inside the smashed window of a wholesale florist's. And a hose that someone had attached to a fire hydrant was just lying there, every once in a while coughing up a half gallon of water like a snake with tuberculosis.

I didn't like the idea of there being people inside, maybe burning to death very quietly. So I pushed through the crowd. I got up to the first floor landing and the smoke there was already too thick and smothery for me to go any higher. But I saw a fireman sitting comfortably against the wall on the landing, his fire helmet slid down over the front of his face. "No beer," he was saying to himself. "No beer and no steam room." I took him by the hand and led him downstairs.

There was a light rain going on, and I felt like getting down on my knees and saying Thank You to the sky. Not that the rain put out this particular fire, but, you know, without the occasional drizzles we had all that day keeping the city damp, there wouldn't have been much of New York left.

Right then, I had no idea that what was going on was limited to New York City. I remember wondering, as I took shelter in a hallway across the street, if all this was some kind of sneak enemy attack. And I wasn't the only one thinking that, as I found out later. I mean the nation-wide alert, and the hot line, and Moscow frantically trying to get in touch with its delegate at the UN. I just read about the treaty the Russian delegate signed that day with the delegates from Paraguay and Upper Volta. No wonder the Security Council had to declare everything that happened at the UN in those twenty-four hours null and void!

When the rain stopped, I began to work my way north again. There was another crowd in front of a big Macy's window on 34th Street near Sixth Avenue. A half-dressed guy and a naked girl were on a couch—the window display was advertising furniture that week—and they were making it.

I stood in the middle of all those trance-like stares and I just couldn't pull myself away. A man next to me with a good leather briefcase kept murmuring, "Beautiful, beautiful. A pair of lemon-green snowflakes." Then the Herald Square clock, the one where those two statues with hammers bang away at a great big bell, that clock began to sound off the strokes of twelve noon. I shook myself and pushed out of the crowd. The guy and the girl were still making it.

A woman on the edge of the crowd, a very pleasant, gray-haired women in a black dress, was going from person to person and taking their money away. She'd take wallets away from the men and little money purses out of the women's pocketbooks, and she'd drop them in a large paper shopping bag. If anyone made the least sign of annoyance while she robbed him, she'd leave him alone and go on to the next one. The shopping bag was hanging kind of heavy.

She suddenly realized I was watching her, and she looked up. Like I said, we non-zombies recognized each other in a flash all that day. She blushed a deep blush, all the way to the roots of her gray hair. Then she turned and ran away at top speed, her heels going clack-clack-clack, the pink slip under her black dress flashing up and swirling around. She held on to the shopping bag as she ran.

The things people must have been pulling that day! Like those two Hoboken guys who heard on the radio that Manhattan had gone crazy. They put on a couple of gas masks and drove through the Holland tunnel—this was maybe an hour before it was closed to all vehicular traffic—and went down to Wall Street to rob themselves a bank. They weren't even carrying weapons: they figured they'd just walk in and fill their empty suitcases with cash. But what they walked into was a street gun duel between two cops from a radio car who'd been hating each other for months. I saw a lot of things like that which I can't remember now while I'm testifying.

But I do recall how the tempo seemed to be picking up. I'd headed into Broadway, giving up completely on the idea of going to the office. There were a lot more traffic accidents and a lot more people sitting on curbs and smiling into space. And going through the upper thirties, I saw at least three people jump out of windows. They came down in a long blur, *zonk-splash,* and nobody paid any attention to them.

Every block or so, I'd have to pull away from someone trying to tell me about God or the universe or how pretty the sunlight was. I decided to, I don't know, kind of withdraw from the scene for a while. I went into a lunch-eonette near 42nd Street to get a bite to eat.

Two countermen were sitting on the floor, holding hands and crying their hearts out. Five girls, secretary-types, were bent over them like in a football huddle. The girls were chanting, "Don't buy at Ohrbach's. Ohrbach's is expensive. Don't buy at Ohrbach's. Ohrbach's is expensive."

I was hungry: by this time that sort of thing didn't even make me sweat. I went behind the counter, found pack-aged bread and cheese, and I made myself a couple of sandwiches. I ignored a bloody knife lying near the bread-board. Then I sat down at a table near the window and opened a couple of my cans of soda.

There were things to see—the tempo was picking up all

the time. A schoolteacher trotting by with a wooden class-
room pointer in her hand, waving it and singing *Little
Red Wing*. Behind her about twenty or thirty pudgy eight-
year-olds carrying bus stop signs, one bus stop sign to
every two or three kids. An old woman trundling half a
dozen dead-looking cats in a brand-new, bright green
wheelbarrow. A big crowd marching along and singing
Christmas carols. Then another, smaller crowd singing
something else, I don't know, a foreign national anthem, I
guess. But, you know, a lot of singing, a lot of people
suddenly doing things together.

When I was ready to leave, another light drizzle started, so I had to sit tight for an hour or so more. The rain
didn't stop the five secretary-types, though. They snake-
danced out into it, yelling, "Everybody—let's go to Fifth
Avenue!" They left the crying countermen behind.

Finally, it was clear and I started off again. All over the
street there were clumps of people, arms locked, yelling
and singing and dancing. I didn't like it one bit: it felt like
the beginnings of a riot. At the Automat near Duffy
Square, there was a bunch of them spread out on the
sidewalk, looking as if they were having an orgy. But
when I got closer, I saw they were only lying there caress-
ing each other's faces.

That's where I met those newlyweds who'll be testifying
after me—Dr. and Mrs. Patrick Scannell from Kosackie,
Indiana. They were standing outside the Automat whis-
pering to each other. When they saw I didn't have the
pop-eyed, zombie look, they fell all over me.

They'd come into New York late the night before and
registered at a hotel. Being, you know, honeymooners,
they hadn't climbed out of the sack until almost two in the
afternoon. That's what saved them. Months before, when
they'd been planning their honeymoon, they'd bought
tickets to a Broadway show, a matinee, Shakespeare's
Macbeth, and they'd charged out of the hotel room fast

not to miss it. They'd run out without breakfast or anything, just a candy bar Mrs. Scannell was carrying in her purse.

And from the way they described it, that production of *Macbeth* was like nothing else anybody ever saw on land or sea. Four actors on the stage, only one of them in costume, all of them jabbering away in speeches from *Macbeth, Hamlet, A Streetcar Named Desire, Oedipus Rex* and *Who's Afraid of Virginia Woolf?* "It was like an anthology of the theater," Mrs. Scannell said. "And not at all badly done. It hung together in a fascinating way, really."

That reminds me. I understand a publishing house is bringing out a book of the poetry and prose written in New York City on this one crazy LSD day. It's a book I sure as hell intend to buy.

But interesting or fascinating or what, that oddball show in a professional Broadway theater scared the pants off them. And the audience, what there was of it, scared them even more. They'd walked out and gone looking around, wondering who dropped the bomb.

I shared my soda with them, using up the last of the six-pack. And I told them how I'd figured out it was in the water. Right away, Dr. Scannell—he was a dentist, I found out, not a medical doctor—right away, he snapped his fingers and said, "Damn it—LSD!" I bet that makes him the first man in the country to guess it, right?

"LSD, LSD," he repeated. "It's colorless, odorless, tasteless. One ounce contains 300,000 full doses. A pound or so in the water supply and— Oh, my God! Those magazine articles gave someone the idea!"

The three of us stood there drinking our soda and looking at the people screaming, the people chuckling, the people doing all kinds of crazy things. There were mobs now heading east and yelling, "Everybody to Fifth Avenue. Everybody to Fifth Avenue for the big parade!" It was like a kind of magic had spread the word, as if the whole population of Manhattan had gotten the same idea at the same time.

I didn't want to argue with a professional man, you know, but I'd also read a lot of those magazine articles on LSD. I said I hadn't read about people doing some of the things I'd seen that day. I mean, I said, take those crowds chanting like that?

Dr. Scannell said that was because of the cumulative feedback effect. The *what?* I said. So he explained how people had this stuff inside them, making them wide open psychologically to begin with, and all around them the air was full of other LSD reactions, going back and forth, building up and up. That was the cumulative feedback effect.

Then he talked about drug purity and drug dosage— how in this situation there was no control over how much anyone got. "Worst of all," he said, "there's been no psychological preparation. Under the circumstances, any-thing could happen." He stared up and down the street at the crowds going chant-chant-chant, and he shivered.

They decided to get some packaged food and drink, then go back to their hotel room and hole up until it was all over. They invited me along, but, I don't know, by this time I was too interested to go into hiding; I wanted to see the thing through to the end. And I was too scared of fires to go and sit in a fourteenth-floor hotel room.

When I left them I followed the crowds that were going east as if they all had an appointment together. There were thick mobs on both sides of Fifth; across the avenue, I could see mobs of people coming west toward it. Every-one was yelling about the big parade.

And there really was a parade, that's the funny part. I don't know how it got organized, or by whom, but it was the high point, the last word, the ultimate touch, to that damn day. What a parade!

It was coming up Fifth Avenue against the one-way traffic arrows—although by this time there was no traffic anywhere—it was coming up in bursts of fifty or a hundred people, and in between each burst there'd be a thin line of stragglers that sometimes wandered off and got mixed in with the people on the sidewalk. Some of the signs they carried were smeary and wet from being recently painted; some of them looked very old as if they'd been pulled out of a trunk or a storage bin. Most of the paraders were chanting slogans or singing songs.

Who the hell can remember all the organizations in that parade? I mean, you know, the Ancient Order of Hibernians, the CCNY Alumni Association, the Untouchables of Avenue B, Alcoholics Anonymous, the NAACP, the Anti-Vivisection League, the Washington Heights Democratic Club, the B'nai B'rith, the West 49th Street Pimps and Prostitutes Mutual Legal Fund, the Hungarian Freedom Fighters, the Save-the-Village Committee, the Police Holy Name Society, the Daughters of Bilitis, the Our Lady of Pompeii Championship Basketball Team. All of them.

And they were mixed in together. Pro-Castro Cubans and anti-Castro Cubans marching along side by side, singing the same mournful Spanish song. Three cops, one of them without shoes, with the group of college students carrying placards, "Draft Beer, Not People." A young girl wearing a sandwich sign on which was scribbled in black crayon, "Legalize Rape—Now!" right in the middle of a bunch of old men and old women who were singing "Jay Lovestone is our leader, We shall not be moved . . ." The County Kerry band playing "Deutchsland Über Alles" followed by the big crowd of men in business suits, convention badges in their lapels, who were teaching two tiny Italian nuns to sing, "Happy birthday, Marcia Tannenbaum, happy birthday to you." The nuns were giggling and hiding their faces in their hands. And behind them, carrying a huge white banner that stretched right across

Fifth Avenue, two grizzled-looking, grim-faced Negro men about seventy or eighty years old. The banner read: "Re-elect Woodrow Wilson. He kept us out of war!"

All through the parade, there were people with little paint cans and brushes busily painting lines up the avenue. Green lines, purple lines, even white lines. One well-dressed man was painting a thin red line in the middle of the marchers. I thought he was a Communist until he painted past me and I heard him singing, "God save our gracious queen . . ." as he walked backward working away with the brush. When his paint ran out, he joined a bunch from Local 802 of the Musicians Union who had come along holding up signs and yelling, "Abolish Folk Songs! Save Tin Pan Alley!"

It was the best parade I ever saw. I watched it until the Army paratroops who'd landed in Central Park came down and began herding us to the Special Rehabilitation Centers they'd set up.

And then, damn it, it was all over.

ABOUT WILLIAM TENN

Theodore Sturgeon, writing in *If* magazine,
had the following to say:

It would be too wide a generalization to say that *every* sf satire, every sf comedy and every attempt at witty and biting criticism found in the field is a poor and usually cheap imitation of what this man has been doing since the '40s. [But] his incredibly involved and complex mind can at times produce constructive comment so pointed and astute that the fortunate recipient is permanently improved by it. Admittedly the price may be to create two whole categories for our species: humanity, and William Tenn. For each of which you must create your ethos and your laws. I've done that. And to me it's worth it.

William Tenn is the pen name of London-born Philip Klass. He began writing in 1945 after being discharged from the Army, and his first story was published a year later. His stories and articles have been widely anthologized, a number of them in best-of-the-year collections. Currently he teaches writing in the Department of English at The Pennsylvania State University.

The long-awaited national bestseller
is coming in May in paperback!

It all began with
THE CHRONICLES OF THOMAS COVENANT THE UNBELIEVER—
Lord Foul's Bane, The Illearth War
and *The Power that Preserves.*

Now the story of Thomas Covenant continues...

THE WOUNDED LAND

27831 / $2.95

by Stephen R. Donaldson

- 2 months on *Time* bestseller list

"Comparable to Tolkien at his best...a true classic!"
—Washington Post